DEAD HORIZON

RACHEL JONES

First published in 2026 by Rachel Jones

Cover Design by Brendan Arnold *(IG: @brendanarnold)*

Edited by GCD Editorial and Ironwood Editorial

Created proudly by a human, for humans.

To anyone who has ever stared into the void of grief and had the strength to keep moving forward anyway – *this story was written for you.*

"The night is darkest just before the dawn."

— Thomas Fuller (1650 AD)

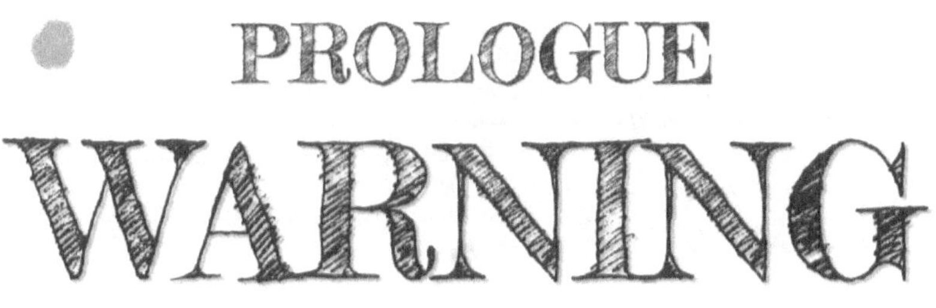

PROLOGUE
WARNING

If you find this note, leave this world.

If you cannot leave – follow the sun.

Night isn't safe.

We were never meant to be here.

—Eva

CHAPTER ONE
ARRIVAL

LOCATION: NG *Astraea – Approaching HDX-2719 System*

16 June, Earth Year 3070

Eva had been raised under artificial light.

Like the generations before her, her circadian rhythm had been tuned not to a sun, but to schedules, when simulated dawns piped gently through the ceilings of the NG *Astraea*.

The ship ran on Earth time, not because it mattered anymore, but because humans needed a fiction of normality to remain sane across an eight-century voyage.

The *Astraea* was never meant to drift forever. From its earliest schematics, it had been designed to descend – to anchor itself into alien soil and become something new. It wasn't just a vessel, but a foundation. A place to live and grow outward from, to build a future that no longer relied on steel corridors and recycled air alone.

Until they could expand into permanent structures, the ship itself would remain their home: atmosphere, power, hydroponics, and life support, carrying thousands of souls inside a ship engineered to endure the unknown. Its corridors bore the quiet marks of those lives – handprints faintly worn into railings, scuffed flooring along the most travelled routes, the occasional flicker of a panel that maintenance crews never quite replaced, only recalibrated over time.

Eva glanced at the panel below the window.

EH + AM BFF

Her initials and Lina's – her best friend since forever – carved when they were only seven.

She smiled, remembering Commander Reyes frowning and telling them off when she caught them in the act. The fact Reyes never ordered the panel to be repaired said something about her – that even the most serious people on this ship had a heart for those living on it.

Eva glanced back up as a gradual bloom of light filled the corridor.

Morning light was always the same – a slow amber spread across the panels, calibrated to mimic a spring sunrise somewhere in the northern hemisphere of a planet none of them had ever seen.

Until today.

Today, there was a real star beyond the hull.

Eva pressed her hand flat against the glass of the forward observation deck, her breath fogging faintly against the windowpane as she stared into the space beyond. The deck around her was quiet at this hour, but in the habitation hubs, doors would be sliding open now. Voices would begin to rise. The low murmur of daily routine – footsteps, distant conversation, the clatter of utensils from the food hall – would soon be threading its way through the ship.

For centuries, humanity had dreamt of this moment. Of arriving in the system just a little early – enough to be among the first to stand beneath a new sun. Children were raised on simulations and dreams, taught that one day their descendants would wake to real light instead of programmed dawns.

And now she was here.

But alone.

Eva glanced to the empty space where her boyfriend Erik had once stood beside her as they'd watched the hazy fuchsia glow of the lightdrift warping around the spacecraft.

'When we get to the planet, I know you'll have work to do,' Erik had begun as he brushed one of Eva's long blonde locks behind her ear. 'But I hope you know that these past two years have been the best of my life. I can't imagine my future with anyone but you.'

She'd giggled as she cuddled closer to him.

'I'm serious, Eva.' He'd gently guided her back a step before lowering himself onto one knee.

Eva had blinked in confusion.

'If you'll have me,' he'd pulled a small glittering ring from his pocket then, 'I want to spend the rest of my life with you.'

Eva had gasped.

'It was my grandmother's,' he'd continued softly. 'And her grandmother's before that, all the way back to Earth. I'm told it's made of gold, set with an opal from a place called Australia.'

'Erik, it could be made from algae rope and I'd still accept it!' she'd cried through a laugh. 'Yes!'

As they'd embraced, the memory faded.

Tears fell down her cheek and soaked into her lab coat as she continued to stare blankly out the window. Somewhere behind her, a door slid open with a soft pneumatic hiss, followed by distant footsteps that didn't come closer – just another sound of life continuing without *him*.

Two years earlier, the *Astraea's* compatibility program had paired Eva and Erik together – one of many matches quietly arranged by the ship's Command to ensure humanity would continue once they reached their new world. The system analysed genetics, psychology, and probability, but it never forced its choices. It simply introduced people who might have fit together.

Eva had almost ignored the notification when it first appeared on her data plate.

Now, she couldn't imagine a version of her life where she had.

As the *Astraea* continued its slow approach, a planet rose beneath her – filling the viewport inch by inch.

HDX-2719-c.

Just over a month ago, the planet had been little more than shifting data and distant light.

Eva remembered the moment the first close-range scans had come through – fragmented and inconsistent. Numbers that didn't quite align with the projections they'd been taught their entire lives.

Then the follow-up briefing reported early signs of solar interference and sensor degradation.

They'd spent weeks arguing over it – running models, recalibrating equipment, trying to reconcile centuries of certainty with information they couldn't fully trust.

No one had said it outright, but the conclusion had been made that they couldn't truly know what waited for them until they saw it for themselves.

And now they were here.

A burnished sphere of gold, crimson, and deep green turned slowly beneath them, cloud bands curling like delicate brushstrokes across its atmosphere. Sunlight caught on the curve of its horizon, scattering into pale halos where air met vacuum.

Eight hundred and seventy-five years of lightdrift. Travelling at five percent the speed of light, thirty-two generations had been born, lived, and died within the *Astraea* – all for this.

'Look at her,' Aelina Morcant whispered beside Eva.

Eva turned just enough to catch Lina's reflection in the glass. Her best friend's eyes were wide and bright, glistening with awe, her usual composure stripped away. Lina was a biologist by training. Precise and methodical, she spent her career classifying life, and yet Eva knew how deeply Lina loved the animals she studied. She always had.

Now, Eva watched as Lina stared at the planet like a child tasting sugar for the first time, wonder written openly across her face.

'She's beautiful,' Lina breathed. 'She looks so... alive.'

Eva laughed, the sound sharp with nerves and joy, and clasped Lina's shoulder. 'She *is* alive,' she said, unable to stop herself from grinning. 'That's the point!'

All around them, the observation deck hummed with quiet chaos.

Children clung to their parents, pointing at the curve of the planet with unfiltered awe. Elders stood apart in silence – men and women born believing they may never feel the touch of soil beneath their feet.

Humanity had left Earth in the year 2195, at the height of the Evacuation Accords. Climate collapse had been the main cause – rising seas, failing ecosystems, entire regions rendered uninhabitable. But Earth hadn't just been dying – it'd been changing.

Destabilised biomes. Mutated microorganisms. Emergent pathogens that spread faster than containment protocols could be developed. Life was adapting at a pace humanity could no longer predict or control.

So they had built the New Generation ships and sent them away, carrying not just the first crew, but seeds, embryos, data archives, animals, and the guilt of knowing that Earth couldn't be saved.

Eva had grown up with this knowledge the way earlier generations of Earth had grown up with stories of wars or fallen empires. The destruction of Earth was embedded into the *Astraea's* foundational education – taught alongside language, physics, and biology – repeated so often it became less a history lesson and more a moral one: a record of how humanity had failed itself.

She knew the images by heart: flooded cities, broken coastlines, forests collapsing into dust.

For Eva, Earth was nothing more than a case study – a warning of what could go wrong.

She had grown up in Hydroponics, her childhood spent beneath towering leaf canopies and nutrient mist that coated her skin with the scent of chlorophyll. Plants had been her constant companions – besides Lina, of course.

These days, her world still centred on Hydroponics, but as they travelled closer to the HDX-2719 system, the botany department had been merged with the xenobiology team. Together they had grown into one of the most efficient scientific units aboard the ship. Mira handled atmospheric and microbial analysis with almost obsessive precision, while Tomas could run modelling faster than the ship's AI system could compile the results. They had worked together long enough that conversations rarely needed finishing – one hypothesis flowing seamlessly to the next.

Lukas Taylor, head of the xenobiology division, was brilliant though deeply unpleasant. His theoretical work had proven invaluable to the mission, but Eva found working alongside him extremely difficult. He had a habit of asking personal questions in moments where they had no place, and his gaze lingered on her just a little too long to be mistaken for casual observation.

Her tablet chimed softly in her hand.

FINAL SYSTEM APPROACH TO HDX-2719 CONFIRMED

STAR CLASS: K-TYPE ORANGE DWARF – HDX-2719

Across the observation deck, murmurs rose in overlapping waves as other crew checked their own tablets. Someone laughed aloud near the far window. A small group had gathered around a projection of the star, pointing excitedly as if seeing it might somehow make the moment more real.

For generations, the *Astraea* had travelled towards a star no living human had ever seen up close before.

Now, it floated in the space beyond the glass.

Eva barely registered the movement until Lina stepped up beside her, their shoulders brushing lightly as she leaned forwards to look out across the view.

'Still doesn't feel real,' Lina murmured, folding her arms against the glass.

Eva didn't answer straight away.

Together, they watched as the planet beneath them rotated slowly.

Too slowly, Eva thought.

Behind them, voices carried through the deck.

'Can you believe it?' someone whispered.

'We're actually here.'

'My grandmother used to tell stories about this day...'

Lina huffed a quiet breath. 'All that build-up and we just... float here staring at it.'

Eva snickered and felt a flicker of something warm stir in her chest – the same hope everyone else seemed to radiate so easily.

But the feeling faltered almost as soon as it formed.

The awe didn't settle the way she'd thought it would. If anything, it made the absence beside her feel sharper.

Her fingers curled slightly against the glass.

We made it.

And yet, Erik wasn't here to see it.

For a moment, something hollow opened in her chest. A quiet, dangerous thought she didn't want to follow.

What's the point of any of this... if he isn't here?

Eva swallowed hard, forcing the thought down before it could take shape.

'That's still bothering me,' Lina murmured, scrolling through her tablet. 'Seventy-two-hour rotation... that's not a minor deviation.'

Eva frowned slightly. 'You think it's a problem?'

Lina hesitated. 'I think... it's something we didn't predict.'

Eva glanced back at the planet. 'The original surveys were done from twelve light years out. Nine hundred years ago.' She exhaled softly. 'There was always going to be margin for error.'

Earth-based astronomers had identified one promising candidate all those centuries ago – a world flagged simply as HDX-2719-c – *Planet C.*

It was the third planet in the HDX-2719 system.

HDX-2719-a was a small, rocky world locked too close to its sun, scorched beyond habitability. HDX-2719-b fell only marginally within the Goldilocks Zone – technically viable, but designated a secondary option at best.

HDX-2719-c, however, had everything.

Breathable atmosphere. Liquid water signatures. Tolerable gravity. A place humanity could begin again. But the final approach had stripped away assumptions as they entered the outer reaches of the system.

Data replaced theory in real time.

Axial tilt – steeper than projected.

Orbital period – faster than expected.

Eva expanded the environmental model, her brow tightening as the projection stabilised.

'Three weeks of daylight,' she said quietly.

Lina glanced over. 'And night?'

Eva hesitated. 'Seven days.'

Lina exhaled slowly. 'That's... longer than I expected.'

'Same,' Eva said. 'I'm curious about what life would emerge from this sort of cycle though.'

A chime echoed through the deck, cutting Eva off as the overhead lights dimmed slightly – a signal that Command had priority.

'COMMAND BRIEFING IN FIVE MINUTES,' a rough female voice echoed over the ship's speakers. 'ALL DEPARTMENT HEADS REQUIRED IMMEDIATELY.'

'We'd better go,' Lina said, folding her tablet back into the pocket of her lab coat. 'Reyes will be pissed if we're late... again.'

They left the observation deck and joined the flow of crew moving through the main corridors. Conversations spilled through the passageways – speculation about the colony site, arguments about atmospheric composition, someone already planning the first celebration on real soil, but Eva barely registered any of it. Her attention drifted past bulkheads marked with caution striping, past maintenance hatches she'd walked a thousand times – until she felt it: a pair of eyes on her.

Lukas.

He leaned against a doorway panel with casual arrogance, slim and pale, a sly smirk tugging at one corner of his lips. Eva's stomach knotted. His presence simply made her skin crawl.

Not long ago, she'd uncovered the truth: he'd tried to wedge himself between her and Erik, pretending to care about "team dynamics", when in reality he wanted her for himself.

She forced her gaze elsewhere, pretending to inspect some important data on her tablet as her fingers tightened around it. She'd shut him down months ago, told him flatly she would never be with him, and yet he never stopped trying.

Noticing this, Lina gave her shoulder a reassuring squeeze, whispering, 'Ignore him.'

Eva exhaled, letting some of the tension ease as they moved forwards, but she couldn't shake Lukas' gaze. Out the corner of her eye, she felt it trail her, slow and deliberate, scanning her from head to toe.

They turned into the Command hub, light spilling out to meet them. Eva and Lina took their seats on the other side of the room, as Commander Reyes appeared before them, posture rigid, expression carefully neutral. Lukas had already slouched into his assigned seat at the back, chin resting on one hand, watching Eva the same way a predator studied its prey.

'All right, I assume you've all had a chance to review the updated planetary data,' Reyes began. 'Before we proceed, there's an operational matter that requires clarification.'

The room stilled.

'Two weeks ago, when the *Astraea* crossed into the outer edge of the HDX-2719 system, we encountered solar radiation levels significantly higher than initial projections.' Reyes brought up an image of the sun, data bands flaring amber and red. 'The exposure caused a cascade of system faults – primarily affecting access, short range sensors, and ship-wide communications.'

Eva's pulse thudded in her ears.

'Critical doors defaulted to sealed protocols. That includes airlocks.' Reyes' jaw tightened. 'Those systems have since been patched. Comms and doors are now operational. Long range sensors remain partially degraded and Engineering is working continuously.'

Reyes paused, her gaze sweeping the room before settling briefly, but deliberately on Eva.

'We lost personnel during that failure,' she said, her tone measured, but quieter now. 'Including Erik Calder, one of our First Class officers.'

Eva's fingers curled slowly into her palms. Her breath hitched and shuddered before she forced it steady again, locking her jaw as she fixed her gaze somewhere past the display.

Don't cry... Don't cry...

'His actions in the face of system failure prevented further loss of life. You have my condolences, Doctor Hall.'

Then, just as quickly, Reyes straightened, the moment closing as discipline reasserted itself.

Eva stared at the screen Reyes now pointed to, her vision blurry as she saw the highlighted airlock icon blinking faintly on the display.

The airlock...

Erik.

She felt it all settle into her chest – not as a scream, not as tears, but as something dense and suffocating. Her throat tightened, but she kept her face still, her hands folded neatly in her lap.

'Despite these complications,' Reyes said, shifting the display, 'conditions on the planet remain within survivable parameters. We'll proceed with primary settlement in the *Aurelion Basin*, as outlined in the original mission statement.'

A section near the planet's subsolar latitude illuminated.

'This zone receives maximum sunlight during this half of the orbit. The objective is stability,' Reyes concluded. 'Final descent operations have begun. Atmospheric entry is scheduled within the next twenty minutes.'

As the trajectory was adjusted, a low vibration rippled through the deck – subtle but unmistakable. The final movements of a ship that had been Eva's entire world.

She barely registered the meeting's end. Standing on instinct, she avoided Lukas and followed Lina out, and only when they reached the corridor did her composure finally falter. Her breath shuddered once – sharp, silent.

Lina caught her immediately, a steady hand at her elbow, guiding her towards the observation window.

This is why, Eva realised. *Why the doors locked. Why there was no override. Why he—*

Anger flared, sudden and cutting.

'They talk about survivable parameters like we're numbers in a model,' she muttered. Her hand curled against the glass, the other tightening around the necklace at her throat – a gold ring set with gleaming opal.

'Erik was nothing to them,' she said bitterly. 'They stood there in perfect rows, said a few rehearsed words, and launched an empty coffin into the dark like it meant something.' Her voice faltered. 'They honoured the uniform he wore. Not the man.'

She pressed her palm against the window, grounding herself in the feel of the cool glass as she steadied herself.

Outside, clouds and atmosphere streamed past as the surface of the planet resolved beneath them – vast expanses of arid desert broken by sweeping bands of green forest that followed the planet's natural contours. Even from orbit, the forests seemed impossibly dense – an unbroken canopy that swallowed the land beneath it.

The *Astraea* made its descent, movement rippled across the plains. Herds of unfamiliar animals scattered in coordinated waves, fleeing the ship's shadow as it carved across the land – a colossal intruder announcing itself to a world that had never known steel.

Eva watched them run.

'Our ancestors made this journey to escape the horrors of Earth,' she murmured, her voice brittle at the edges. 'They said this place was the future.'

She exhaled, then turned slightly towards Lina. 'I'm sorry. I know I'm being—'

Lina shook her head before she could finish, stepping closer. Her hand tightened around Eva's. 'You don't have to apologise,' she said quietly. 'Not for this.'

Eva nodded, swallowing. After a moment, she leaned into Lina, resting her forehead briefly against her shoulder. 'Thank you,' she whispered. 'For always being here.'

Lina smiled softly. 'Always.' She nudged Eva lightly. 'Come on. Let's go see the world he helped us reach.'

Lina and Eva made their way to one of the airlock chambers and watched the ramp lower with a hiss of pressure. The inner hatch opened, exposing the outside as the dust settled around the ship and dark soil stretched beyond.

Eva tapped her foot impatiently. Partially because she wanted to see this new planet, but she also didn't want to spend another minute in an airlock.

Finally, a small team moved first.

Clad in full environmental suits, they stepped carefully onto the surface, scanners already active. One knelt, pressing a sensor into the soil, while another swept the air, watching readouts flicker across their tablet. A third monitored radiation levels.

Quiet – almost – besides the crunching of boots against soil, and the steady clicking of the Geiger counter.

Eva and Lina followed with the second team, helmets sealed, tablets in hand. Eva's gaze flicked between the horizon and the stream of data scrolling across her own screen – real time data of atmospheric composition, pressure, particulate density.

A voice crackled over the comms. 'Atmosphere within tolerable range. No immediate toxins detected.'

Another pause.

'Radiation nominal.'

'Safe to remove helmets, everyone!' someone called from the first team.

Around them, seals released with soft clicks as helmets came off, one by one.

Nodding, more to herself than anyone else, Eva exhaled slowly, eyes scanning her tablet one more time. The readings aligned.

'It's stable,' she murmured.

She hesitated only a second longer before disengaging hers. The seal broke with a quiet hiss, and she lifted the helmet free.

She drew her first breath and moved her feet, feeling the ground give slightly beneath her boots, softer than she'd expected.

For a moment, she didn't move.

Real ground.

Not reinforced deck plating. Not polymer walkways or the impermeable corridors of the *Astraea*.

The air tasted different too.

The recycled atmosphere aboard the ship had always been clean, carefully balanced, but sterile in a way that was difficult to describe. This air carried texture. Heat. A faint dryness that lingered on her tongue when she inhaled, mixed with a strange earthy bitterness she couldn't quite place.

Eva drew another breath, slower this time.

Her lungs expanded a little more easily than they had aboard the ship, the gravity of this world pulling just slightly differently against her body. The sunlight felt warm as well – not the gentle amber wash of the ship's artificial dawn, but something harsher and more direct, pressing against the back of her neck.

For the first time in her life, there was no ceiling above her. The sky stretched endlessly overhead, turquoise, pale, and enormous. It made her feel strangely exposed, as if the universe had suddenly grown much larger around her.

A flicker of awe moved through her chest – the same quiet wonder she'd imagined as a child whenever the *Astraea's* teachers spoke about the day humanity would finally arrive.

But it tangled with something heavier.

Erik should be here.

He should've been standing beside her, laughing in disbelief like everyone else, pointing out features on the horizon the way he always did during simulation drills.

Instead, the space beside her felt unbearably empty.

Eva swallowed and forced herself to take another step forward.

Ahead, a broad stretch of vegetation spread across the *Basin* – dense, layered growth forming a natural boundary between desert and forest. Tall, fibrous cacti-looking plants swayed gently in the breeze, their needles catching the light in shades of deep crimson and burnished gold.

Beside her, Lina had stilled.

Beyond the vegetation, movement flickered – shapes shifting between trunks and shadow. Creatures watched from a cautious distance, antlered silhouettes and glinting eyes half hidden among the trees.

'Do you see them?' Lina whispered, barely containing her awe.

Eva nodded, though her attention was quickly refocused on the plant life around her, on the way the leaves responded subtly to the light, how the variety of life here was beyond her wildest dreams.

But the grief was still there, sitting heavy in her chest, unyielding.

Erik had died to get them here.

For that sacrifice to mean something, she would have to keep going.

Whether she was ready to or not.

CHAPTER TWO
DUSK

LOCATION: *The Greenbelt*
23 June, Earth Year 3070
LOCAL CYCLE STATUS: *Dusk – two hours before nightfall*

The *Greenbelt* extended beyond the edge of the *Aurelion Basin* like a wall, dense with layered green growth that was almost beyond comprehension. Giant trees rose in braided spirals, and along the bark ran dark patches of verdant moss. Fronds from some of the ground cover foliage unfurled in slow, deliberate arcs, responding to the setting sun with a precision that made Eva's hands itch to catalogue every variation she came across.

They had settled the ship down and anchored into the ground just over two weeks ago. Eva worked for hours, sometimes beyond her allocated time, boots sinking into dirt that smelled faintly sweet and mineral-rich.

The days on *Planet C* still felt wrong to her body.

For generations, life aboard the *Astraea* had followed carefully regulated cycles – artificial dawn, artificial dusk, every hour measured and predictable. Here, the sun lingered in the sky for weeks at a time, barely shifting along its slow arc before it had begun its gradual descent towards twilight.

Eva often lost track of time entirely.

Her body expected a night that never came. Sometimes she felt exhausted while the sky blazed with turquoise daylight, while other times she lay awake inside her room long after the rest period alarms chimed – reminding the colony to relax – her mind stubbornly alert beneath the constant glow outside.

Human rhythms had evolved for a world that turned every twenty-four hours.

But until her body learned this planet's strange cycle, work was easier than trying to rest.

She pulled out the notebook that she'd tucked beneath her arm.

Actual paper.

It was an unnecessary weight, vulnerable to moisture, fire, loss – but Eva preferred it. She trusted ink more than data. Paper didn't crash. It didn't corrupt. It didn't vanish with a power surge.

And it felt real.

The sheets were cultivated in Hydroponics, where waste stems, leaf husks, and pruned biomass were broken down, then pressed and cured in thin layers by automated rollers older than Eva's great grandparents.

The process was slow, the paper rationed and tracked – reserved for ceremonial records and defence personnel. Eva had been taught to make it during her apprenticeship, guided by her mother who believed that knowledge deserved to be passed down through generations.

She knelt near a low growing fern, its green fronds edged with almost translucent filaments that shimmered faintly in the sunlight, and grabbed a sample before writing out her notes.

Specimen 041: Provisional Classification.

Photosynthetic response is unusually efficient under the K-type light spectrum.

Growth is clustered near a form of decaying biomass.

Non-aggressive.

She paused, tapping the pen against the page.

'Non-aggressive,' she murmured, then hesitated before adding a small question mark beside it.

Erik would have teased me for that, she thought.

The memory rose unbidden – his voice warm, amused, always steady.

'Write what you see. Not what you hope it is,' he'd said.

Eva exhaled slowly. How was she meant to be responsible for classifying alien flora? How did one even begin to comprehend life that hadn't evolved alongside humanity.

Her fingers tightened around the pen, the paper rasping softly beneath her grip.

She hadn't always written like this. On the *Astraea*, she'd used data tablets like everyone else – quick entries, clean files, backed up and forgotten. It was Erik who had taught her to slow down. To anchor herself in life – and in the fragile traditions of the people that came before them.

'If the systems fail,' he'd said once, pressing a notebook into her hands – a six-month anniversary gift from his personal stash, 'you'll still have this.'

She'd laughed then, breathless and disbelieving. 'You realise *I* make these, right?' she'd said, incredulous.

His smile had been soft, certain. 'And so, *obviously* you should be allowed one!' He'd laughed.

Light splintered through the forest canopy, smearing green and gold as Eva's legs gave way beneath her.

She hugged the notebook tight against her chest as she grasped her necklace, the gold ring pressing cold against her palm.

The airlock.

A flagged destruction protocol – low risk, routine. Plant matter from Hydroponics that had tripped an anomalous bio-scan. Nothing dangerous, not officially. Still, protocol demanded its destruction and Defence oversight present until clearance was granted.

The tiny plant sat encased in a biohazard container on the trolley she'd rolled into the airlock chamber.

Eva had thought the whole process excessive.

Erik had disagreed.

'Procedures exist because people get complacent,' he'd said, flashing her that crooked smile as he reached for the inner door controls.

Then the alarms had screamed without warning.

Pressure alerts had flashed across the chamber displays. Red warning lights strobing violently, washing the airlock in pulsing colour.

Eva had frozen.

A system fault warning had blazed across the panel beside the door.

INNER SEAL FAILURE

The words had barely registered before the pressure gauge began to drop.

Her heart had slammed against her ribs.

She'd grabbed Erik's arm.

'There's only one life suit,' she'd said, her voice already shaking.

'I know.'

He'd pulled the emergency suit from its wall mount, placing the helmet in her hands before she could protest.

'I can reset it manually,' he'd said.

Calm. Too calm.

'I've done the drills. You'll be okay.'

'That's not—' Her voice had cracked as the realisation tore through her. 'You won't last fifteen seconds!'

He'd kept moving, pulling the suit over her shoulders with quick, practiced motions.

Then he'd smiled.

Not bravely. Just... knowingly, as if he had already accepted his fate.

He had locked her mag boots to the deck and sealed the helmet over her head. Strands of her hair caught in the collar ring as his hands settled at her shoulders, steadying her.

'I love you,' he'd said. 'Forever and always.'

Before she could answer, he'd flipped the reset switch.

The chamber had roared as the outer seal disengaged.

Air had torn from the room in a violent rush, wrenching Erik from the deck as though something enormous had seized him. His body had vanished through the open hatch in an instant, swallowed by the vacuum beyond.

Eva had screamed his name, reaching for him long after he was gone.

Her vision blurred.

The forest around her – vibrant and alive – dissolved into colour and motion as she wept. The notebook remained clutched to her chest as her breath hitched, ink bleeding faintly across the page where her pen had stalled too long.

She didn't hear Lina approach. She only felt arms around her shoulders, solid and warm, anchoring her back into the present.

'Oh, Eva,' Lina whispered, crouching beside her to pull her gently upright. 'You don't have to do this alone.'

Eva's fingers tightened in the fabric of Lina's sleeve.

'How do you mourn someone you loved,' she asked hoarsely as tears poured down her cheeks, 'when you never had the chance to say goodbye?'

Lina didn't answer right away. She just held her, pressing her forehead to Eva's temple, while the forest breathed around them – indifferent to the human visitors within.

A shadow passed overhead.

Eva and Aelina looked up just in time to see a form of flying insect sweep low through the canopy – its wings spanning nearly two metres, translucent fiery red and deep orange membranes catching the sunlight like stained glass as it banked through the canopy.

'*Meganeura ignis*,' Lina breathed, lifting her recorder briefly before lowering it again. 'Very similar to Earth's dragonflies! They seem to be getting bigger the deeper we move into the Greenbelt.'

The air vibrated faintly with the beat of its wings, a subtle hum that seemed to make the surrounding fronds twitch in anticipation.

Then, impossibly fast, a plant reacted. A long, sinuous stalk whipped from the undergrowth, tipped with serrated leaves glinting like shards of obsidian. Eva barely had time to blink before it struck the creature, the canopy trembling from the sudden, violent impact.

What Eva had assumed was a passive, bowl-shaped plant that she'd catalogued as "Specimen 034" earlier in the week – now retracted, its deep purple petals snapping shut around the insect's thorax. Barbs locked together, puncturing membrane and chitin alike.

The sound was... crunchy.

She froze, a humming pulse roaring in her ears as the insect screamed – a high, shrill sound that cut off abruptly as the plant constricted.

Within seconds, it was over.

The plant settled back into the first floor, its outer surface pulsing faintly as digestive fluids went to work.

Eva forced her grief to the back of her mind.

'*Carniflora titanica*,' she whispered, wiping her tears on the back of her sleeve as she wrote quickly in her notebook.

Appears to be attracted to vibrant colours.

She hesitated, then added:

Observed feeding behaviour appears selective. No aggression towards humans.

'C'mon, let's get back to the ship,' Lina said as she linked her arm with Eva's.

As they approached the *Astraea*, Eva's gaze drifted to the *Sunlace Vine* – a plant she had discovered on the first day after landing. Its thin, spiralling stems curled like delicate hearts, climbing eagerly towards the light, leaves shimmering a bright, almost electric green. Somehow, seeing it here, flourishing despite everything, made her chest tighten and ease at the same time.

She imagined Erik would have liked it. A faint warmth lifted her sorrow, just a little, as if the vine carried a piece of him forward with her. Commander Reyes had approved a few to be planted at the entrance, and now, as the light shifted and shadows stretched across the ground, the vine seemed to glow in the softening dusk, a small, stubborn defiance against the encroaching dark.

Beyond the entryway, slim sensor pylons stood half-buried in the soil – part of the external array deployed in the first week. Atmospheric monitors, seismic readers, and audio pickups fed a constant stream of data back into the *Astraea*, a quiet network listening to a world no one yet understood.

Her wrist monitor chimed – a clear, sharp tone – joined almost immediately by Lina's.

AUTOMATED COLONY NOTICE:

SOLAR OUTPUT SHIFT DETECTED

STATUS: DUSK IMMINENT

RETURN TO BASE IMMEDIATELY.

Around her, a few colonists glanced towards the dimming horizon. Someone laughed.

'So it begins,' a nearby technician said, the humour thin, nerves threading his voice despite his smile.

At first, it was subtle – a slow draining of colour from the sky, the red and gold paling as if a veil was being drawn slowly across the sun. Over the span of a minute, the shadows lengthened, stretching unnaturally across the ground.

Then the land shuddered.

A booming, galloping thunder rolled through the *Basin* as the soil trembled beneath their boots. Eva turned just in time to see movement rippling along the edge of the *Greenbelt*.

Herds of *Spectrocervus septemcornis* – the "ghost deer", as Lina had named them – burst from the forest edge, pale forms flashing between the trees. They ran in wild, panicked clusters, antlers clipping branches, hooves tearing through undergrowth in blind urgency, as if fleeing something unseen.

They didn't slow.

They didn't look back.

The herd split as it ran. The young stumbled as they tried to follow their mothers. The old faltered, crying out in thin, reedy calls that went unanswered. One limped blindly before vanishing beneath the pounding tide of hooves, leaving behind a still corpse.

Eva felt her stomach tighten.

By the time the last of them disappeared into the distance, the light had dimmed further – not yet night, but enough that Eva felt it settle in her chest, a quiet certainty that something was wrong here.

No one spoke as they turned back towards the ship.

The mess hall was louder than usual.

Voices overlapped in bursts of laughter and conversation, trays clattering, chairs scraping across the floor as crew filled the space in restless waves. The descent had shifted something in everyone – anticipation, nerves, and excitement.

Eva and Lina sat tucked into their usual corner of a long shared table, half-surrounded by familiar faces.

Lina's aunt Kara was two seats down, arguing animatedly with one of the hydroponics techs over nutrient ratios, her hands moving just as much as her voice.

'If you overcorrect the nitrogen balance this early, you'll destabilise the entire cycle—'

'—it's called adapting, Kara. You should try it sometime—'

A snort of laughter came from across the table. Someone else muttered, 'Here we go again.'

Lina leaned closer to Eva, lowering her voice. 'Five credits says Aunty Kara throws something at her in the next thirty seconds.'

Eva huffed a quiet laugh, the tension in her chest easing just slightly.

Across from them, a young technician – *Jalen*, she thought; she'd never been great with names – was pushing food around his tray, barely eating. His knee bounced under the table, a nervous rhythm that didn't match the energy around him.

'You good?' Lina asked, nodding towards him.

He forced a quick smile. 'Yeah. Just... feels weird, right? Finally being here?'

Eva gave a small nod as she leaned closer to Lina. 'Didn't animals on Earth scatter before disasters?' Eva murmured, her voice low over the hum of the mess hall.

Lina paused mid-bite, chewing slowly before she answered. 'Sometimes. From what I learned – earthquakes, volcanic events, floods. Animals seemed to know before humans did.'

Eva stared down at her tray. The food had gone cold.

'This feels... the same,' she said quietly. 'But different.'

Lina frowned, tapping her fork against the edge of the plate. 'On Earth, animals fled because something physical was coming. They could possibly feel pressure changes. Or heat? This—' She hesitated. 'I don't know.'

Eva hummed softly in response.

'Or maybe they migrate in ways we don't understand yet. Follow the sun?' Lina gestured vaguely with her fork. 'We've barely scratched the surface of this place.'

Eva nodded as the words lingered.

Follow the sun.

'You two are going to ruin a perfectly good dinner with all that doom talk.'

The voice cut in warm and dry.

Eva looked up.

Commander Reyes stood at the end of the table, one hand braced lightly against the back of an empty chair. Up close, she looked less like the rigid figure in charge of a whole colony and more like someone who hadn't properly rested in days.

'We're just being scientifically observant,' Lina said, lifting her fork defensively. 'We're scientists, you know!'

Reyes arched her brow. 'Oh yes? Is that what we're calling it?'

A ripple of quiet amusement passed around the table.

Kara leaned back in her chair. 'You tell them, Commander. They're spiralling.'

Reyes glanced between them, her gaze settling briefly on Eva.

'It's normal,' she said, her tone quieter now. 'What you're feeling. What you're all feeling.'

The table stilled.

'You've just stepped onto a world no human has ever set foot on,' she continued. 'Your instincts are trying to make sense of something they've never encountered. That doesn't mean something is wrong.'

Eva held her gaze. 'And if it is?' she asked quietly.

For a fraction of a second, something unreadable passed across Reyes' face.

Then it was gone.

'Then we'll face it,' she said simply. 'Together.'

She straightened slightly, the leader in her slipping back into place.

'Get some rest where you can,' Reyes added, her tone lighter again. 'Once the daylight cycle begins, I expect all of you to be too busy complaining about real problems to invent new ones.'

A few people chuckled.

Kara muttered, 'If anyone wants to complain about my food, you know where my fist is.'

Reyes almost smiled.

Then she moved on, continuing through the mess – stopping at other tables, exchanging brief words, a steady presence moving through the noise.

Eva watched her go.

'She makes it sound easy,' Jalen said under his breath.

Lina shrugged. 'That's kind of her job.'

Eva didn't respond.

Her gaze lingered a moment longer on Commander Reyes.

Because for the first time—

She wasn't entirely sure she believed her.

By the time night fell, Command had sealed the *Astraea*.

Eva stood just inside the main access doors as the final locks engaged, heavy mechanisms clamping shut with deep, resonant thuds.

Officially, it was simply a precaution. Protection against the dark unknown of an alien world.

Unofficially, everyone felt it.

The air inside changed – recycled, controlled, safe. Just as if they were in space again – while outside the *Aurelion Basin* and the *Greenbelt* beyond it darkened into something unknown.

Eva stood at one of the reinforced viewports and watched the Milky Way shimmer in the indigo sky. She squinted into the horizon to see if she could see anything move, but the animals were gone.

They'd all fled.

She noticed then in the *Greenbelt*, soft pink bioluminescence drifting upwards from the undergrowth, rising in lazy spirals.

They clung briefly to bark, to the grass reeds, and to the shape of the poor animal that had been left behind earlier – glowing bright against the encroaching dark.

Eva pressed her hand to the glass. 'They have to be some sort of spore release,' she whispered to herself. 'They're incredible.'

'Dangerous things often are.'

She stiffened before turning.

Lukas appeared beside her, arms folded, gaze fixed on the drifting lights. He hadn't announced himself. He never did.

'Imagine what we could learn,' Eva said, carefully neutral. 'If we could sample them properly.'

'I could go sample—' Lukas said at once.

'The seals are closed,' she interrupted.

'I know,' he said quickly, a smile flickering into place. 'But I thought—'

'No.' Eva straightened, her tone crisp. Professional. Final. 'Absolutely not.'

For a moment, something unreadable passed over his face – hurt, maybe. Or frustration. Then he lifted his hands in surrender.

'I was only suggesting,' he said lightly.

Eva turned back to the window, forcing her mind elsewhere. She reminded herself he was a brilliant xenobiologist, meticulous and cunning with samples, the kind of mind that could make discoveries others would miss. And yet... the way he watched her, always, the way his interest in her seemed tangled with something dark and invasive, made her skin crawl. She wanted to respect his skills but not his presence.

She remembered the way he'd looked at her when Erik was declared MIA. The sympathy had shifted into something else. Something possessive. Something that set her teeth on edge.

'Some things,' she said quietly, 'are better studied from a distance. Especially when we don't know what the night cycle brings here.'

Outside, the pink orbs thickened – gathering, drifting closer – as the last true daylight bled from the sky.

CHAPTER THREE
EMERGENCE

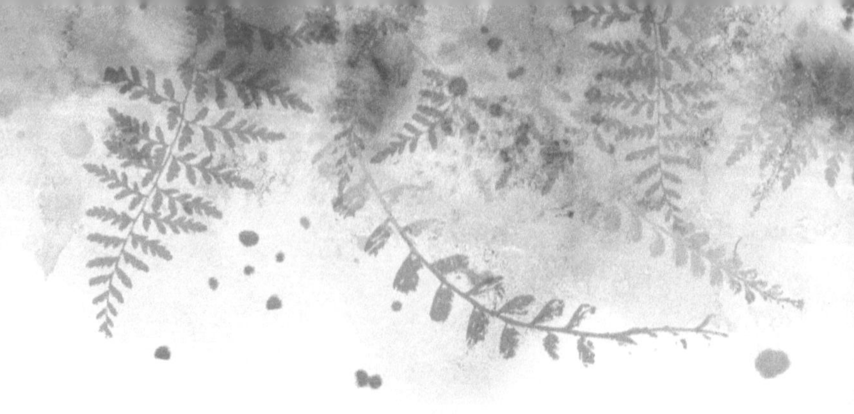

LOCATION: *NG Astraea – Aurelion Basin*
24 June, Earth Year 3070
LOCAL CYCLE STATUS: *Night One*

A ghost deer lingered near the edge of the *Greenbelt* – one of the juveniles abandoned by its herd and left to fend for itself. It seemed drawn towards the ship by curiosity, hunger. It wandered close to the entrance, pale and uncertain, investigating the strange new life that had taken root at the boundary of its world.

Its white hide gleamed faintly in the spill of the interior lights, seven antlers rising from its skull like branching bone as it lifted its head and breathed in the night air.

Eva watched as the pink spores drifted towards it, slow and graceful. They reminded her of the old Earth images – snowfall captured in silent recordings, flakes tumbling lazily to the ground.

Like snow, they settled first along the deer's muzzle. Then its eyes, dissolving on contact, melting into the soft tissue as if absorbed by warmth alone.

Lina stood beside her, bouncing with excitement. 'This is as close as we've been able to get to them so far!'

Eva smiled gently at her best friend's enthusiasm and lingered long enough to convince herself there was nothing here for her to note down. She turned, already thinking about the lab – about unfinished classifications.

'I'm gonna head back to the—'

A high-pitched scream tore through the corridor speakers – sharp, piercing, and wrong in a way that froze the blood.

Eva flinched, spinning back to the windows, convinced a colonist had been hurt.

But no one in the corridor was moving.

They were all staring out the windows.

Eva peered through as the same shriek sounded again – distorted slightly now through the external feeds.

The ghost deer.

Its body convulsed violently, legs buckling as it thrashed against the earth. Hooves carved deep, frantic scars into the soil, kicking up dirt and vegetation as the sound tore from its throat – wet, broken, wrong.

Blood burst from its nostrils first, thick and dark, then streamed from its eyes, spilling down the delicate white fur in jagged paths. Its mouth opened in a final, strangled cry as crimson poured free, soaking its chest, its legs, and the ground beneath it.

Gasps rippled through the observation corridor.

Someone retched. Another colonist stumbled back from the glass, hand clamped over their mouth, whispering *no, no, no* under their breath. A child began to cry before being dragged away by a parent.

The deer staggered once, its antlers striking the soil with a dull, hollow crack, then collapsed. Its body shuddered, spasmed, and went suddenly, unnervingly still.

The silence afterwards was worse than the screaming.

Lina made a small, broken sound beside her.

Eva turned just in time to see her best friend's face drain of colour, eyes wide and glassy, fixed on the lifeless form outside. Lina's hands trembled as she pressed them to the glass, as if she had some force within her to undo what they'd just witnessed.

'It was healthy,' Lina whispered, voice cracking. 'It was fine. It hadn't even reached maturity—'

Her breath hitched, words unravelling into helpless disbelief.

'It was a baby – just left behind – a baby...'

Eva stepped closer, gently pulling Lina's hands away from the doors. 'I know,' she murmured. 'I've got you. Just don't look.'

Lina clutched at her, shaking now. 'It didn't suffer long,' she said desperately, as if trying to convince herself. 'It was fast. Too fast.'

Eva didn't answer at first. She rested her forehead briefly against Lina's shoulder, listening to the tremor in her breathing.

'Do you remember Nibbles?' she asked softly, searching for something to pull Lina's mind away from the sight outside.

Lina blinked, confused. 'What?'

'The rabbit,' Eva said softly. 'The one we found in the intake vents in Hydroponics. The one that chewed through half the lettuce crop when we were seven.'

For a moment, Lina didn't respond. Then she gave a weak, breathy exhale. 'I remember,' she said. 'You mean the one you insisted we keep instead of reporting?'

'It wasn't his fault,' Eva murmured. 'He was just trying to survive. Same as everything else.'

Outside, the deer's body lay motionless in the dust.

Lina's grip on Eva tightened. 'Commander Reyes was furious,' she said faintly.

'She still is,' Eva replied, a ghost of a smile touching her voice. 'I don't think she's ever forgiven us.'

Lina let out a shaky breath that might have been the beginning of a laugh, or a sob.

The drifting spores settled across the deer's ruined body in slow, deliberate clusters – as if the carcass itself was drawing them in.

On the second night aboard the *Astraea*, the complaints started.

A dull headache someone mentioned in passing. A cough that lingered a moment too long in the corridor outside the lab. People rubbing beneath their eyes as though the lights had suddenly grown too bright.

Eva didn't think much of it at first. Colonists had been moving constantly since landing – new air, new microbes, and long hours. But by the end of the shift, she began to notice the pattern.

Too many people reaching for painkillers that did nothing to ease the strain. Too many tired eyes and tense voices.

It was most obvious in her own team.

Mira missed a plant classification review – unheard of from her. Tomas showed up late, eyes bloodshot, apologising as he swallowed two tablets dry. Someone else laughed then pressed a hand to their forehead as if pained by the sound.

'You alright?' Eva asked Tomas, frowning.

'Just allergies or something,' he said, forcing a smile as he dabbed at his nose with his sleeve. 'Guess the recycled air has finally gotten to me.'

Eva nodded, though unease stirred low in her stomach. The *Astraea's* atmospheric systems had been tuned and retuned for centuries – adaptive filters, microbial scrubbers, airflow patterned to mimic open spaces. Illness still happened, of course, but not like this. Not all at once.

Her gaze drifted across the lab.

Lukas stood at the back, half shadowed beneath one of the light panels. His cheeks were flushed, breathing shallow and fast, dark hair damp at his temples as if he'd been running hard. When he noticed her watching, he startled – a sharp, almost guilty reaction – before recovering too quickly. He smiled and lifted a hand in greeting.

Eva frowned, keeping her eyes on him as he dragged his sleeve across his brow, wiping away the sweat. Lukas had never been one for physical exertion – he preferred theory, simulations, anything that kept his hands clean. Seeing him like this set something prickling low in her spine.

It wasn't the sweat. It was the timing. The way he wouldn't quite meet her eyes. The way his smile felt... rehearsed.

She thought of the weeks after Erik's death – the practised concern, the sudden proximity, the way Lukas had mistaken grief for an opening. How she'd shut him down, and how he'd smiled then too, promising to return when she was "feeling better", as if *she* had wronged *him*.

That same smile now.

Where have you been?

The question rose, then sank again as Lina touched her elbow, pulling her back into the room.

'They've called a Command briefing,' Lina said quietly. 'Department heads.'

Eva exhaled. 'Why?'

Lina shrugged. 'Something about irregularities. They didn't say what.'

Eva cast one last glance back at Lukas, but he had already turned away, heading towards one of the other connected labs.

'Let's go,' Eva said.

They moved into the corridor flow. The *Astraea's* passageways branched in clean, familiar lines, guiding traffic between zones without thought. The laboratories occupied the ship's midsection – a dense lattice of interconnected rooms dedicated to botany, xenobiology, ecology, and medical research. Glass walls glowed softly as they passed, casting pale reflections across the corridor.

As they passed the communal food hall and kitchens – usually the loudest place on the ship – the air still carried the scent of nutrient stews, but the voices tonight were muted, conversation low and uncertain. A man leaned against the wall near the entrance, rubbing at his temple with two fingers, eyes squeezed shut.

As they continued rearward, the corridors widened, giving way to reinforced bulkheads marked with hazard striping. Storage bays and fuel cells lined this section, sealed behind thick doors built to withstand the vacuum. The deeper they moved into this part of the ship, the more the ambient hum from the engines sounded – lower, heavier – vibrating faintly through the floor beneath Eva's boots.

She drew in a slow breath.

The air felt... strange. Not wrong. Just, different.

She let it out again and kept moving.

The escape pod bay lay just beyond, its inner doors sealed as always during transit. Eva barely spared it a glance – though, for the first time in a while, she found herself suddenly aware of it.

Near the far end, an elevator shaft rose through the ship's spine, carrying personnel upward into the Command ring.

Eva stepped inside beside Lina as the doors sealed.

For a moment, nothing happened.

Then the lift engaged with a low, juddering hum.

Eva's brow furrowed as she exchanged glances with Lina, but the motion smoothed out almost immediately, carrying them upward.

The ascent pressed faintly beneath her feet as the ship fell away below, carrying them towards Command – and whatever waited there.

As they entered, voices were low and clipped, conversations ending abruptly as they took their seats. People stood closer together than usual, shoulders nearly brushing. Commander Reyes stood elevated on the central platform, her posture rigid. The main display behind her cycled through surveillance feeds and diagnostic overlays, orange alert markers flashing intermittently across several sectors of the ship.

'We've identified a potential breach risk,' she said. 'This meeting is precautionary. Nothing more.'

Eva felt a chill run down her spine.

Precautionary.

The word, whatever it meant, didn't sit right.

'We're reviewing all logs from the last twenty-four hours,' Reyes continued. 'Until then, I need confirmation from each department head.'

Her gaze settled on Eva. 'Doctor Hall. To your knowledge, was any external seal opened in the botany labs after dusk?'

Eva didn't hesitate. 'No,' she said. 'All admittance to the lab is accounted for. No external doors have been accessed.'

Even as the words left her mouth, something in her chest tightened.

Lukas – earlier. The way he had looked at her. The way he hadn't been acting quite... *right.*

A flicker of doubt surfaced, but she pushed it down immediately.

Reyes nodded at her, eyes moving on.

Around the table, voices echoed the same answer.

'No.'

'Negative.'

'Not to my knowledge.'

Reyes folded her hands behind her back. 'There have also been reports of minor physiological symptoms among several crew members – headaches, dizziness, mild nausea. At present, medical staff are monitoring closely.' Her jaw tightened almost imperceptibly. 'Furthermore, there is an additional matter concerning newly updated planetary data,' she said carefully. 'Information that will require *full* departmental briefing.'

A subtle shift rippled through the room.

'However,' Reyes continued, her tone firm, 'our immediate priority is containment, system verification, and crew welfare. Further analysis is ongoing, and speculation at this stage would be unproductive.'

Reyes' gaze swept the chamber.

'A briefing will be scheduled once your team's assessments are complete. Until then, all departments are to remain focused on their assigned tasks.'

The meeting adjourned with instructions to monitor ongoing symptoms and reduce nonessential movement.

As they filed out, Eva felt the unease deepen – not because of what had been said, but because of what hadn't.

Back in the corridor, Lina slowed, glancing down the hall. 'I should probably go find Aunty Kara,' she said. 'She's in the kitchen again tonight, and if things are getting weird around the ship, I'd rather she wasn't dealing with it alone.'

Eva nodded. 'Sure. I'll be in the lab if you need me.'

Lina smiled tiredly. 'You and your little plants.'

She pulled Eva into a quick hug before heading down the corridor towards the food hall.

Eva watched her go for a moment, then turned in the opposite direction.

She still had weeks of classifications to log.

But as she walked, she found herself thinking about the briefing. About the updated planetary data. About the ghost deer. And even about Lukas, and the way he made her skin crawl without ever quite crossing a line that she could report.

And beneath it all, Erik.

The way the loss of him still arrived in quiet, uninvited waves when she let her mind drift for too long.

But at least the classifications made sense. Numbers, patterns, structure. Things she could control.

She picked up her pace towards the lab.

Suddenly, the idea of work felt like the only thing keeping her sane.

CHAPTER FOUR
BREACH

LOCATION: *NG Astraea*

25 June, Earth Year 3070

LOCAL CYCLE STATUS: *Night Three*

Eva found comfort in names.

They anchored things. Gave shape to the unknown. Reduced chaos into something that could be studied, understood, and contained.

She stood alone in her lab, light panels dimmed to night cycle levels, the hum of preservation units steady and familiar around her. Specimens floated in clear suspension cylinders, labelled and catalogued in neat rows – the first living records of this world.

She activated her console and pulled up the current log.

Campsis aurora

Common Name: Sunlace Vine

She barely paused. The description had already been written: green tendrils unfurling like delicate strings, drawn instinctively towards the direction of the sun.

She marked the classification as confirmed and moved on.

Phragmites susurro

Common Name: Whisper Reed

A tall, hollow-stemmed grass native to the nearby marshlands. When disturbed by wind, it produced a low frequency resonance – a hum that seemed to pierce the air, spooking anyone nearby.

Eva added a brief note beneath the entry.

Psychological impact on colonists observed. No biological threat identified.

She lingered, fingers hovering above the keyboard.

She'd felt it too when gathering a sample. A faint vibration through the soles of her boots, through bone. It was like the planet murmuring to itself.

She dismissed the thought and continued.

Apiaceae carota

Common Name: Ashroot

Found in the dusty plains of the *Aurelion Basin*. She rotated the preserved sample. Thick, dark skinned, carrot-like roots adapted to nutrient poor soil.

Her gaze drifted to the final entry in the log.

No label yet. Just a temporary tag: *Specimen 041*.

Eva leaned closer.

Its fronds were suspended mid unfurl, faintly luminous veins branching through the green like frozen lightning. Even preserved, it emitted a soft glow – not enough to light the room, but just enough to be noticed.

There was something about it she couldn't quite figure out. Even preserved and encased in an airtight jar, it carried the unsettling impression of persistence – as if the sample was still alive somehow.

She logged its scientific classification *Polypodiophyta luminis* – Lumen Fern – her fingers moving automatically, and flagged it for further study.

She straightened, rolling the tension from her shoulders.

Enough for now.

She pinged her team for a general staff meeting.

They arrived in twos and threes, moving slower than usual – the same group that normally filled the lab with overlapping reports and quiet competition over who could classify samples fastest. No one joked. No one lingered. Mira kept a blood-darkened cloth pressed beneath her nose, eyes glassy with pain.

Tomas opened his tablet, stared at it for several seconds, then frowned as though he'd forgotten why he'd picked it up.

Another coughed – a dry, shallow sound that scraped the air and echoed too loudly in the lab's sterile quiet.

Eva waited until they were settled.

'I know some of you are unwell,' she said, keeping her voice calm and measured. 'Thank you for coming in regardless. This won't take long.'

She ran through safety protocols first, and asked for updates on ongoing classifications, pending analyses, anything that might be time sensitive.

The answers came back fragmented. Incomplete.

Normally her team moved through these briefings with effortless precision, but tonight, that rhythm was gone.

People paused mid-sentence, losing their train of thought. Data reports came haltingly, details forgotten or repeated twice. A team built on careful observation was struggling to concentrate.

'Before everyone leaves,' Eva said, 'I need to ask something directly.'

A few heads lifted. Mira's fingers tightened around the cloth.

'Has anyone here opened an external seal?' Eva asked. 'At any point. For any reason.'

They exchanged looks – confusion first, then a flicker of offence.

'No,' Mira said immediately. 'Of course not.'

'Absolutely not,' Tomas added, voice hoarse.

The others shook their heads, murmuring agreement.

Eva studied them carefully. She saw discomfort, fatigue, pain – but not guilt. 'Alright,' she said. 'That's all. Go rest. Report any worsening symptoms immediately to the medical team.'

They filed out one by one.

Only Lukas remained.

He stood near the far bench, hands braced against the surface as if grounding himself. He hadn't moved since the meeting ended.

'Lukas?' Eva said. 'Did you need something?'

He didn't look at her when he said, 'I didn't mean for this to happen.'

Her stomach dropped.

'For *what* to happen, Lukas?' she asked carefully. 'What did you do?'

He swallowed hard, finally lifting his head. 'It was me,' he said. 'I broke the seal.'

The words sucked the air from the room.

'What?' Eva breathed.

His voice shook. 'I—I had to know what those pink orbs were out there. You said yourself you wanted to know.'

A brittle laugh escaped him as he stepped closer, reaching for her hand as if familiarity might soften the damage.

'I did it for you... I'd do anything for you...'

For a heartbeat, she almost didn't see Lukas at all.

She saw Erik instead – hands steady, movements precise as he guided her into the life suit just weeks ago. The way he'd whispered his love for her before stepping back – giving his life so she could have hers.

The memory snapped away – sharp and bright, like a blade.

Eva stepped back instantly.

'Lab quarantine. Now.'

Her fingers flew across the console, initiating containment protocols. Doors slammed down with mechanical finality. Warning lights flared amber, then red.

She turned back to Lukas, heart hammering.

'Sit down. Don't move.'

She opened a secure channel to Command.

'Commander Reyes, do you copy?'

No response.

She tried again.

'Commander – we have a breach.'

Silence.

The lab lights flickered.

Somewhere beyond the sealed doors, a scream tore through the corridors, raw and ragged.

Eva swiped the console open and punched in her management access codes. The surveillance program hummed to life, feeds from every sector of the *Astraea* appearing across the screen.

She found the source of the screaming first. A woman knelt in the corridor, mere metres down the hallway, her hands clawing into her skull. Blood streaked down her arms, dripped onto the floor, painting it a deep, glistening red. Her body shuddered violently as she rocked back and forth, eyes wide, unseeing. Eva's throat tightened.

A shiver ran through her spine. She forced herself to breathe, trying to focus on the next feed. Another colonist stumbled into view, coughing violently, crimson soaking his sleeve. Beside him, someone else collapsed completely, convulsing. The screams multiplied, bouncing off the sterile metal walls, echoing endlessly.

Eva's fingers hovered over the controls, reluctant to look away but knowing she had to see the full scope of what was happening.

Something was very, very wrong.

Eva leaned against the console, her hand still covering her mouth as her mind raced.

'Eva! Let me in!'

She spun around.

Lina stood at the sealed door, breathless, pale – but upright.

'You shouldn't be here,' Eva said, already moving towards the door. 'If there's something in here, some kind of contagion—'

Lina shook her head sharply. 'Have you been outside the lab in the last hour?' she asked. 'Deactivate the quarantine. Trust me, I can explain.'

'I can't.' Eva shot a glare back at Lukas. 'He's the one who broke the seal Command was talking about. He could be contaminated. I won't risk you like that.'

'Lukas?' Lina said flatly, her own glare slicing through the glass. 'Figures.' She exhaled. 'It doesn't matter anymore. Whatever this is – it's already all through the ship.'

Eva swallowed hard, glancing back at the monitors.

Then she keyed in the override.

The seal disengaged with a heavy hiss, and alarms shut off. Lina stepped inside, and the door slid shut behind her.

She scrubbed a hand across her face, breathing unevenly.

'I couldn't find Aunt Kara anywhere,' Lina muttered. 'She was supposed to be working kitchen rotation tonight.'

Eva reached out, resting a steady hand on Lina's arm – the only comfort she could offer.

'She might've locked herself in somewhere safe,' Eva said quietly. 'A lot of people seem to be doing that.'

Lina nodded, though the tension in her shoulders didn't ease. 'Yeah, maybe,' she said quietly. 'But I had to keep looking, so I went for a walk.'

Eva felt her chest tighten.

'That's when I saw people who'd only been a little off earlier,' Lina continued. 'Headaches. Nausea. But now, they're just... lying in the corridors. In their rooms. Some of them weren't moving at all.' Her voice faltered. 'There was blood everywhere, Eva. On the walls. On the floors. Everywhere...'

Eva's gaze flicked over Lina instinctively – searching for something she hadn't thought to notice before.

Blood. Skin. Eyes.

Nothing.

'You're not coughing,' Eva said quietly. 'No bleeding. No—'

Lina stilled. 'Neither are you.'

Behind them, someone screamed again over the monitors.

'So why aren't we being affected like them?' Lina whispered.

Eva's gaze drifted back to the monitors.

Deck identifiers flickered across the feeds – habitation hubs, hydroponics levels, cargo access corridors. The same scenes repeated in different configurations. Blood-slick walls. People dragging the injured into sealed rooms. Doors locking behind them.

It wasn't influenza. That had been eradicated centuries ago.

It wasn't environmental stress alone.

There were too many symptoms.

Too much blood.

For the first time since Lukas had spoken – since the alarms, the screams, the impossible images – the spinning stopped.

And the anger took hold.

Lukas stepped forward. 'Look, Eva, I'm sor—'

'Shut your *fucking* mouth!' Lina snapped. 'You caused this, you slimy little shit.'

'I just wanted to make Eva happy—'

Eva spun on him. 'You could *never* make me happy,' she yelled. 'You could *never* replace Erik. *Ever*.'

Lukas' hand hovered for a moment, fingers twitching, as if he wanted to touch her shoulder. His eyes didn't leave hers. A bitter laugh escaped him, low and sharp.

'You think I care about replacing Erik?' he sneered, stepping closer. 'You're so blind, Eva. I *know* what we could be...'

Eva recoiled, shoving herself back against the console. 'Don't. Come. Near me.'

He didn't stop. His smirk twisted, half frustration, half something unreadable and dangerous. 'I'd do *anything* for you. I'll protect you… all you have to do is—'

Before he could reach farther, Lina's hand shot out, pushing firmly against his chest. 'Fuck off, Lukas,' she snapped, voice sharp and unwavering. 'Back the hell up.'

He stumbled slightly at the force of her shove, a flash of frustration crossing his face, but he didn't retreat entirely – just lingered, eyes flicking between Eva and Lina.

'You didn't do this for me,' Eva snapped, her voice like ice. 'Whatever you brought inside this ship – this is on you.'

For a tense moment, he stared, as if calculating the next move, before his shoulders slumped just slightly. He backed to one of the adjoining labs, eyes still on her, a silent warning in his gaze.

Eva's chest heaved and her hands clenched. Erik's name burned in her mind, raw and aching.

'I'm not going anywhere,' Lina said quietly, stepping closer. 'Don't worry – we'll figure this out. Together.'

CHAPTER FIVE
REANIMATION

LOCATION: *NG Astraea*

26 June, Earth Year 3070

LOCAL CYCLE STATUS: *Night Four*

Eva's fingers stilled against the console.

Jonas Keiffer, systems analyst, had always been quiet and methodical – the kind of person who corrected data tables in silence and stayed late to ensure redundancies were logged. Eva had never heard him raise his voice in the eight years she'd known him.

Now, he was screaming.

The feed from the habitation corridor flickered to life on the console. Jonas staggered down the hall, hands clawing at his skull as if some invisible force was ripping him apart from the inside. Blood streamed from his eyes and ears, dripping onto the floor in dark, chaotic streaks. His steps were jerky, uncoordinated, like a machine losing its calibration.

Lina swore under her breath, 'What the fuck is he doing?'

Colonists scattered, some shouting, some frozen in place. One woman tried to approach him, reaching out in desperation – only to recoil as Jonas slammed his head into the wall, again and again. The hollow impact echoed through the speakers, reverberating through Eva's chest.

'Jonas—stop—' Eva leaned forward instinctively, one hand braced against the console like she could somehow reach through the screen and pull him back.

Bone gave way as Jonas' body collapsed in a heap, neck broken, blood pooling beneath his head and spreading outward in a dark, widening stain.

Lina recoiled sharply. 'What the f—'

The woman screamed and collapsed to the floor with him, cradling his head in her lap.

Lina's voice dropped, tight and shaken now. 'That's Monica... his wife.'

Eva didn't know what to say.

She stood rigid, fidgeting with the gold ring on her necklace, staring at the feed as others pressed themselves against the walls or fled down branching corridors.

She should have been moving. Doing something. Saying something that mattered.

What would Erik do?

Instead, she stood there, frozen.

Lina dragged a hand down her face, pacing once, then back again. 'Where the hell is medical? Why isn't anyone—' She cut herself off, looking back to the screen, jaw tight.

It sickened Eva – not just the blood, or the violence, but the knowledge that she was powerless. These were her people. Colleagues. Friends she had eaten with, argued with, trusted. And whatever this was tearing through the *Astraea*, there was no protocol for it. No treatment plan. No reassuring lie to offer to them.

She wasn't that sort of doctor. She couldn't triage. Couldn't sedate. Couldn't ease the pain unfolding in real time. Her training told her how to preserve specimens, how to catalogue life – not how to save it.

The medical team should have responded by now...

No orders from Command.

The channels were silent.

Every unanswered call felt like a door slamming shut in her face.

Eva swallowed hard, shame and fury twisting in her chest.

I don't know what to do!

She could name plants down to their cellular structures. She could explain spore migration, evolutionary adaptations – but she could do nothing, absolutely nothing, as everything she knew unravelled before her.

Then Jonas moved again, but not like before. Slowly. Stiffly. Limbs jerking as though pulled by invisible strings. His head lolled at an impossible angle, a wet, jagged crack snapped through the feed as he pushed upright from Monica's embrace.

His eyes opened. Milky and bloodshot – whatever looked out through them was no longer Jonas Keiffer.

'Jonas?' Monica called out.

He swayed and oriented, unaware of anything at all.

'Jonas?'

He turned towards his wife and lunged.

The feed dissolved into chaos. Bodies scattered. Someone fell. A scream cut short into a wet, choking sound as Jonas bit down, teeth tearing into Monica's flesh with animal precision.

Eva tore her gaze away, bile burning her throat.

'Oh my god,' someone whispered behind her.

Eva spun around. She hadn't realised how many people Lukas had gathered in the lab until now.

Do something!

Lina's hand found Eva's shoulder. 'We need to contain this,' she said, obviously reading the panic in her friend's eyes. 'Activate quarantine protocols now. We isolate this section before it spreads.'

Eva's fingers flew across the console, opening the lab's emergency interface. Warning lights flared as the system attempted to seal corridors, but the response was sluggish. Sector after sector failed to lock down as doors refused to engage.

'Only a few labs around us will hold,' Eva whispered, jaw tight. 'We can create a small safe zone here... and manually override doors if we find anyone else nearby.'

The system reluctantly responded, locking down the immediate lab cluster. Amber panels glowed around them, sealing them and the surrounding area off from the rest of the *Astraea*.

The feed streamed more horrors: bodies convulsing, blood pooling, screams ricocheting down metal hallways. Eva swallowed hard, forcing herself to focus. They couldn't save everyone – for now, they could only save themselves and those inside this small enclave.

Eva's mind reeled.

Why is this happening? What is causing it?

The answer didn't come – but memory did. A projection screen in one of the *Astraea's* leisure domes. The smell of citrus of a carbonated drink. Erik's shoulder warm against hers as they laughed at the clumsy, exaggerated gore of ancient Earth films.

'Zombies,' she'd said as the credits rolled, amused. 'They really thought this was how the world could end?'

Erik had smiled, thoughtful rather than mocking. 'People are afraid of losing their humanity,' he'd said. 'Of becoming something that hurts the ones they love.'

Always so wise.

A sob broke the air as a woman collapsed to her knees. 'Please,' she begged hoarsely. 'Please don't let me turn into that.'

Others echoed her – splintered, terrified voices overlapping.

She forced herself to move, handing out bottles of water from a nearby fridge to the few survivors who had joined them, and crossing back to the security panel once more, cycling through feeds. Her hands were steady despite the pounding in her chest. She didn't know what she was searching for – only that she had to keep looking.

That's when she saw the exterior access corridor – the one Lukas had breached.

She zoomed in on the door. The status banner glowed a hard, warning red, flashing MANUAL OVERRIDE where a green integrity lock should have been.

Her gaze snapped to Lukas, crouched in the corner of the lab, arms wrapped around himself, eyes fixed on something he held in his hands.

How could you do this?

How could you risk everyone's life like this?

Eva's anger surged.

She remembered every time she'd shut him down, every blunt refusal she'd given him. She'd never, and would never, be with him. Yet he kept trying.

When he peeped up and saw Eva staring at him, he made to shift forwards as if her eyes offered an invitation only meant for him.

'Lukas!' Lina barked, stepping in front of Eva. 'Thought I told you to fuck off.' She pointed to one of the conjoining labs, sending him away.

Lukas hesitated, lips twitching, but for now, he obeyed.

Eva pulled herself together, focusing back on the feeds.

A ghost deer stood there.

Or what remained of it.

Its white pelt was matted and dark with dried blood. One antler hung snapped and jagged, barely attached. Its ribcage jutted unnaturally against the skin, punctured and collapsed.

It should not have been standing.

And yet it hurled itself again and again against the reinforced wall – skull cracking audibly with each impact – driven by nothing but blind, relentless persistence.

Her gaze flicked to Lina, to the terrified faces surrounding her, then to the memory of Erik stepping back into the void so she could live.

She forced the panic down, reaching for the part of herself that had always steadied her – the scientist.

They had run every scan the *Astraea's* medical system possessed. Infection markers. Parasites. Neural pathogens.

There was nothing.

People were simply dying – and then something in their bodies was restarting.

'I think...' she said slowly. 'I think it's airborne. Whatever it is. And it seems to be targeting neural pathways.'

Lina switched her focus from the monitors to her best friend.

'Do you remember Carina-9?' Eva asked suddenly.

Lina's eyes widened. 'Our hybrid trial?'

'We spliced adaptive plant immunity with animal cellular repair,' Eva said, words tumbling faster now. 'It created a virus that reversed malignant growths without destroying the host.'

'We cured cancer, yes, I know,' Lina said.

Eva trailed off, staring at the darkened corridors. '... then something else could have evolved naturally to do the opposite. On an alien world – the possibilities are endless.'

Lina nodded, as her eyes drifted back to the surveillance console – where shadows of the dead kept rising.

CHAPTER SIX
COLLAPSE

LOCATION: *NG Astraea*

27 June, Earth Year 3070

LOCAL CYCLE STATUS: *Night Five*

The Astraea is beginning to fail.

First, the lights.

Eva watched on as entire habitation centres dimmed to emergency amber, then some panels flickered out entirely, leaving corridors fragmented into bands of shadow and light. Motion sensors lagged, activating seconds too late. Doors hesitated before opening, seals whining as if reluctant. The ship's carefully curated stability – eight centuries of redundancies and routines – all began to peel away.

Then communications.

Audio channels crackled, cut mid-sentence, or dissolved into static or cries for help that ended too abruptly.

Oxygen followed.

The air grew thick and stale, tinged with a metallic tang that coated the back of the throat. Carbon scrubbers struggled to compensate. People breathed shallowly, instinctively conserving something they didn't fully understand they were losing.

Some survivors sat slumped against walls or curled on the floor, some rocked back and forth, whispering fragments of prayers to a god many no longer believed in. Most just sat with hands trembling, staring blankly into nothing, waiting for death to claim them.

But not all of them were still.

A woman jerked her arm away when the man beside her shifted too close, her breath catching as she scrambled back against the wall. 'Don't—' she snapped, voice thin with panic. 'Don't touch me.'

'I didn't—' he started, hands raised, but the woman kept shuffling away.

A man in the corner began to sob – deep, shuddering sounds that scraped raw against Eva's nerves.

Another who bled quietly as one of the remaining medics struggled to contain the flow begged quietly for the release of death before it got worse, before he became "one of *them*".

'He's already turning,' someone whispered from across the room.

'Shut up,' another hissed. 'You don't know that.'

'Neither do you.'

The words fell into a brittle silence.

Eva stood at the centre of it all, heart pounding, mind racing, and felt the full weight of it settle onto her shoulders. She'd spent hours cycling through camera feeds, casualty reports, and medical logs, still trying to find a pattern to the madness.

Command isn't coming.

Medical isn't coming.

If anyone was going to act, it would have to be her and Lina.

She turned.

'Weapons are sealed in the Command ring,' Eva said. 'If we're going to survive this... we're gonna need them.'

The *Astraea* had never been designed for internal violence. Weapons were sealed by defence protocols – safeguards against mutiny across an eight-century voyage. No one had ever imagined they would need to defend themselves from the people they'd grown up with. Lived beside. Loved.

'I'm coming with you,' Lina said immediately.

Eva shook her head. 'No. You stay here.'

'Eva—'

'Someone needs to keep this place functioning,' Eva said. 'These doors, the safe-zone systems, the feeds. If something happens out there, you're the only other person who can lock it down or get these people out.'

Lina's eyes shone with fear and grief. Shared lifetimes pressed between them – childhood laughter, whispered dreams, futures they'd always assumed would arrive.

Finally, Lina nodded. 'Don't make me regret letting you go.'

'I promise I'll be back.' Eva whispered as they embraced.

Lukas stepped forward. 'I'll go with her.'

Both women turned.

Lukas stood stiffly, shoulders tense, his face pale beneath the harsh lab lighting. His eyes flicked briefly towards Lina before settling on Eva again – as if he couldn't quite bring himself to hold Lina's gaze.

'I w—won't take no for an answer,' he stammered.

Eva hesitated. After what Lukas had done, every instinct in her screamed to leave him behind – to pretend he didn't exist.

But instinct wasn't going to get her through the ship alive.

She gave a single nod. 'Fine,' Eva said coldly. 'But you follow my lead. One mistake, and I leave you behind.'

He didn't argue.

Lina sealed the doors behind them.

Eva turned for one last look through the glass. Lina lifted her chin, offering a brave, unconvincing smile as she pressed her hand to the window.

Eva had never been apart from her.

Not once.

She raised her own hand, pressing her palm against the cold surface in silent mirror. 'I'll see you soon.'

Eva and Lukas walked down the corridor for the first time in over four nights.

It was empty.

Too empty.

They moved past the habitation centre, boots sliding slightly as blood slicked the floors in long, smeared curves – as if bodies had been dragged, or had dragged themselves, away. Doors stood open, lights flickering weakly inside abandoned pods. Personal effects lay scattered: a dropped tablet looping a half-written message, a child's shoe, a blanket soaked through with dark red.

No bodies.

No people.

A low sound drifted through the ship – distant, rhythmic.

A wet, rasping growl.

Lukas flinched, instinctively stepping behind a support pillar.

'If we stop, we're dead. Keep moving.' Eva glanced at him. 'You volunteered for this, remember?'

He nodded as they moved faster.

The Command ring entry loomed ahead. Eva scanned her access card with shaking hands. The side panel flickered, hesitated—

A harsh buzz.

Denied.

Eva's stomach dropped.

'Shit...' She swiped again, slower this time, forcing her hand to steady. The panel lagged, the screen stuttering with static.

Another growl echoed, closer now.

The light finally blinked green.

The doors slid open, but not cleanly. They dragged, juddering along their track with a strained metallic whine, as though something deep within the system resisted the command.

Eva slipped through first. Lukas followed close behind.

They rode the elevator in silence.

Halfway up, the lift jolted and lights flickered.

Eva's breath hitched as the cabin stuttered – then resumed its ascent with a low, uneven hum.

When the doors finally slid open, cold air spilled out to meet them.

The Command ring was largely untouched – consoles closed down, chairs neatly aligned – except for one station in the corner, smeared with drying blood.

An increasingly familiar sight.

They moved carefully towards the defence hub, checking dark corners, listening for any movement.

Eva's pulse thudded in her ears. Every sound felt amplified – the soft scuff of their boots, Lukas' uneven breathing, the faint electrical buzz of failing systems.

As they walked, Eva found herself remembering the last time she had been here – on a date with Erik.

He'd pulled her through the restricted corridor with a conspiratorial grin, laughing quietly when the security light blinked green for him. He knew he wasn't supposed to bring her there.

'Relax,' he'd whispered, leaning against the sealed defence lockers like he owned the place. 'First-class clearance has its perks.'

She'd laughed and kissed him beneath the sterile white lights, telling him he didn't have to show off for her.

She remembered the smell of him – clean fabric and the faint metallic bite of gunpowder clinging to his clothes from the firing range – the scratch of his beard against her cheek.

The way he'd smiled when she'd touched his face.

But he was gone now. He'd died saving her.

'Here!' Lukas called out.

The memory snapped shut as Eva stepped into the hub behind him.

Eva peeked inside through the small window in the door. Weapons lockers lined the walls.

The door was sealed.

Eva moved straight to the primary console, fingers flying across the interface.

ACCESS: RESTRICTED – AUTHORISATION REQUIRED

She swore under her breath, slapping her access card against the panel over and over.

Behind them, the growling rose again – closer. Wet. Dragging.

Lukas turned, scanning the corridor. 'Eva—'

'Shh!'

The system stalled.

Processing...

Processing...

Eva's jaw tightened as a heavy thud echoed somewhere in the ring. 'Come on—'

ACCESS GRANTED

Locks disengaged with a sharp mechanical clunk.

'Go!' she snapped.

They didn't waste time. They grabbed at anything they could reach that wasn't locked away.

Rifles. Sidearms. Shock batons. Ammunition sealed in vacuum packs. They worked quickly, methodically, stuffing duffle bags until the weight dragged painfully at their shoulders.

Eva's arms burned. Her breath came too fast, too shallow. Sweat cooled against her spine despite the chill in the air.

The growling rumbled throughout the ring again – broken vocal cords forcing air through ruined tissue.

'Eva,' Lukas hissed. 'There's only one way in or out of here. If we get trapped—'

'I know!'

As they rushed out, passing the console stations again, Eva froze.

She glanced around the pristine room again. The Command centre was immaculate, frozen in its routines. No overturned chairs. No signs of panic.

The console covered in blood...

Whoever had been here hadn't fled. They'd stayed at their post – long enough to bleed for it.

Eva crossed the room, wiping dried blood from the screen as she read the action log.

EMERGENCY BEACON ACTIVATED

REYES: VIDEO LOG UPLOADED

PENDING TRANSMISSION TO NG *HERMES*

Her breath hitched.

Another New Generation ship!

With shaking hands, she initiated a data transfer – *Astraea's* logs, environmental readings, medical reports, Command records, everything – and sent it to the lab's console.

'Eva... what are you doing?' Lukas demanded. 'We need to go *now*!'

The progress bar crawled.

70%

89%

The growling moved closer, wet and eager.

'Eva, NOW!' Lukas shouted.

100%

The sounds that had surrounded them stopped, and silence flooded the room.

'Okay, let's go! Move!' Eva yelled as they ran.

They didn't slow until they rounded the corner – and stopped short.

Commander Reyes stepped into their path.

Or what remained of her.

One side of her uniform hung in shredded strips. One sleeve was soaked black with blood. Her eyes were glassy, unfocused, jaw working slowly as if remembering how to chew.

Lukas made to dip around her, but she was faster.

Reyes grabbed him, dragging him down, fingers digging into his arm and nails tearing through fabric and flesh alike.

'Eva—!' Lukas cried out, scrambling, trying to wrench himself free as she dragged him to the floor. 'Help me! Don't just stand there—help me!'

His hand shot out towards her, slick with blood, fingers grasping at her hands, unable to hold on.

For a split second, Eva looked at Reyes.

The way she *wasn't human anymore.*

She took a step back.

'No—no, don't leave me—please, Eva, please!' Lukas' voice broke, raw and desperate. 'You can't just—'

Reyes bit down.

His scream tore through the corridor, cutting himself off as teeth sank into his shoulder, ripping free meat and tendon. Blood sprayed across the wall and Eva in a thick, violent arc.

Lukas choked on the sound, body jerking as she shook him.

Then, through the pain—

He hurled something at her.

A specimen jar.

'They come from the Lumen Fern!' he screamed, voice cracking, frantic now. 'I'm sorry—I'm so sor—'

Reyes tore into him again, when something clattered across the floor – a sharp, hollow sound almost lost beneath Lukas' screams. A security card skidded to a stop near Eva's boot, smeared red, its small yellow status indicator still blinking weakly.

Eva dropped to snatch up the card and the duffle bag in one frantic motion, refusing to look at Lukas' shredded arm that had fallen beside it – bone exposed, fingers still curled as if reaching out for her.

She just ran.

Her boots slipped on the blood-slick floor as she slammed her hand against the elevator controls at the end of the corridor, jabbing the button again and again.

Come on! Come on!

Behind her, the screaming cut off.

Her breath hitched. Against every instinct screaming at her not to, she glanced back.

The *thing* that had once been Commander Reyes had Lukas pinned at an unnatural angle, his body bent wrong, spine torn and visible through ragged flesh. His head lolled, barely attached, jaw slack as Reyes tore into him with brutal, efficient force – teeth ripping, wet sounds echoing as blood dripped to the floor.

The elevator chimed.

The doors slid open and Eva staggered backward into it, never taking her eyes off the corridor. Reyes lifted her head slowly, mouth slick and red, strands of muscle hanging between her teeth – then she dropped Lukas and charged at Eva.

The doors began to close.

Reyes slammed into them, fingers clawing through the narrowing gap, nails screeching against metal as her face filled Eva's vision – eyes glassy, unfocused, jaw unhinging as if she meant to bite straight through the doors.

With a violent wrench of unnatural strength, the doors shuddered and stopped.

Then they began to slide back open as Reyes forced her way through.

Her movements were wrong – jerking, mechanical. Blood coated her uniform in dark, wet layers. Her eyes were dull and unfocused, and her mouth hung open in a feral snarl.

Eva stumbled backward until her spine hit the rear wall.

For a split second, she froze.

Commander Reyes.

The woman who had commanded the *Astraea* ever since Eva could remember. The woman who had presided over graduation ceremonies, colony briefings, ship-wide announcements. The woman who had shaped everyone's lives, including hers.

Now she staggered forward like a broken puppet.

Eva's hands fumbled inside the duffel bag hanging off her shoulder.

Reyes lurched closer.

A flash of memory cut through the panic – the night with Erik, watching the terrible old zombie movies salvaged from the *Astraea's* archives.

'Zombie rule number one,' Erik had laughed. 'Destroy the brain.'

She yanked the sidearm free from the bag as Reyes lunged, then fired.

Gunshots exploded inside the confined elevator, deafening.

The first round tore through Reyes' skull. Bone and grey matter sprayed across the closing doors in a wet burst. The other two shots penetrated her cheek and jaw, the force snapping her head sideways, and her body collapsed, slamming heavily onto the elevator floor in front of Eva.

Eva stood frozen, the pistol trembling in her grip, ears still ringing.

Commander Reyes lay motionless at her feet.

For a moment, Eva could only stare.

'I'm sorry,' she whispered hoarsely. 'I'm so, so sorry.'

The elevator lurched and began to descend.

Then something moved.

Eva's breath caught.

Beneath the torn fabric of Reyes' uniform, something pale and green pushed through the blood-soaked cloth.

A thin tendril unfurled.

Then another.

Small, faintly luminous growths forced their way through ruptured skin, unfurling delicate fronds that shimmered softly in the elevator's sterile lighting.

Ferns.

Eva stared in horror.

The growths were blooming directly from Reyes' ruined body – feeding on her, spreading, slowly opening like a flower towards the sun.

Her stomach turned as more growths forced their way through Reyes' mouth, bursting through her once golden-brown eyes as they took root within the flesh.

Reyes' jaw hung slack, tongue lolling as more pushed past her lips, unfurling slowly upwards as a bloom of luminescent spores released, drifting upwards into the air – faint, glittering motes of pink.

Eva sucked in a sharp inhale, then clamped her mouth shut, turning her face away as her eyes squeezed closed. One arm came up instinctively, shielding her nose and mouth as she pressed herself back against the elevator wall, as if she could make herself smaller – harder to reach.

The spores settled anyway.

She felt them land across her arms and the exposed skin at her throat – weightless, almost cool.

Her heart thundered in her chest, but still, she held her breath.

Seconds stretched as the elevator descended, but nothing happened.

Eva opened her eyes, watching as the drifting spores clung to her skin for a moment longer, before lifting away as if they had found nothing to take root in.

The elevator continued its silent descent.

When the doors opened again, she ran until she slammed her fists against the lab doors, pounding with everything she had left. Lina wrenched them open just in time to drag her inside, the seals whispering as the doors slid shut behind them.

Eva collapsed to the floor, weapons spilling from the duffel bags with dull, metallic clatter. Her breath tore in and out of her chest, every inhale burning. She didn't let go of the specimen jar as her fingers locked white around it, muscles cramping.

Lina dropped to her knees in front of her instantly. 'Eva—'

She didn't answer. She stared into the jar as faintly luminous pink spores drifted in slow suspension – floating like weightless dust.

Exactly as they had in the elevator.

Blood smeared the glass. Lukas' blood – dark and tacky where her fingers had pressed against it.

'Lukas didn't make it,' she said distantly. 'He... held Reyes off so I could get away.'

Lina's hands hovered just short of touching Eva, eyes scanning her face, her throat, her arms.

'Are you hurt?' Lina asked.

Eva blinked slowly. 'No.'

Lina's gaze sharpened. 'Then who gives a fuck about Lukas? Are you sure you're okay?'

Eva hesitated.

The memory hit her all at once—

The spores bursting from Reyes' body.

'Th—' She swallowed. 'The spores.'

Lina went completely still. 'What?'

Eva dragged in a shaky breath, eyes unfocused as she replayed it.

'I tried not to breathe. I shut my eyes, covered my mouth… I thought—' Her voice faltered. 'I thought that was it.'

Her fingers curled tighter around the jar.

'But when I looked… they weren't…'

She frowned, trying to find the right words.

'They didn't land on me. Like—' She shook her head weakly. '—like they weren't interested in me or something…'

Lina's expression shifted, as if a million questions suddenly filled her mind. 'And you feel… normal?'

Eva nodded slowly. 'No headaches. No bleeding. Nothing.'

Lina exhaled, sharp and controlled, then glanced at the jar again. 'Okay,' she said quietly. 'Okay…'

Eva turned back to the jar as she rotated it slightly under the light.

She gestured weakly to the spores drifting inside the jar. 'They come from the fern.'

Lina frowned. 'The fern? What fern?'

'Lukas said... and I saw it,' Eva said. 'The Lumen Fern.'

Lina stiffened. 'Saw what?'

'In the elevator. After I shot Reyes.' Her throat tightened. 'It didn't stop. It grew.'

Lina stiffened. 'Grew... and what's this about Reyes?

'She—she killed him...' Eva said. 'And then—'

She struggled for the words, her mind flashing back to the elevator.

'She wasn't dead, Lina. Not really.'

Eva looked up at her.

Lina's expression tightened, but she didn't react with shock.

'You're okay,' she said gently. 'Now tell me, ferns grew from where?'

'From inside of her,' Eva said. 'It's like—' She looked up, eyes glassy. 'Like we're the soil.'

Silence.

'Spores from the fern enter our system,' Eva continued, sitting up and piecing it together as she spoke. 'Skin. Lungs. However they can. But it's slow in humans... slower than what we saw outside with the ghost deer.'

She grabbed the bottle of water that Lina offered her. 'Our bodies fight it.'

'Our immune response fights back.' Lina nodded. 'That would explain the early symptoms, the headaches... and so on.'

Eva sipped from the bottle before her voice dropped.

'Until it can't anymore.'

They both fell silent.

Then Lina asked the question that Eva knew had been plaguing them both since the beginning.

'Then why are we still standing?'

Eva looked down at her hands.

Lukas' blood still stained her skin.

Blood.

'Maybe...' Eva said slowly, 'because of our blood.'

Eva's gaze drifted back to Lina when something tugged at her memory – small and insignificant at the time.

A routine medical check where she and Lina had laughed together when they learned they shared the same blood type.

Eva looked up suddenly. 'You're O negative, right?'

Lina blinked. 'Yeah...'

Eva's breath caught. 'So am I, remember?'

They stared at each other.

Understanding flickered – uncertain, fragile, but there.

'No dominant antigen markers,' Lina murmured, half to herself now. 'Nothing obvious for a foreign organism to bind to...'

'Exactly.'

Lina stood and helped Eva to her feet. 'Looks like we have some research to do.'

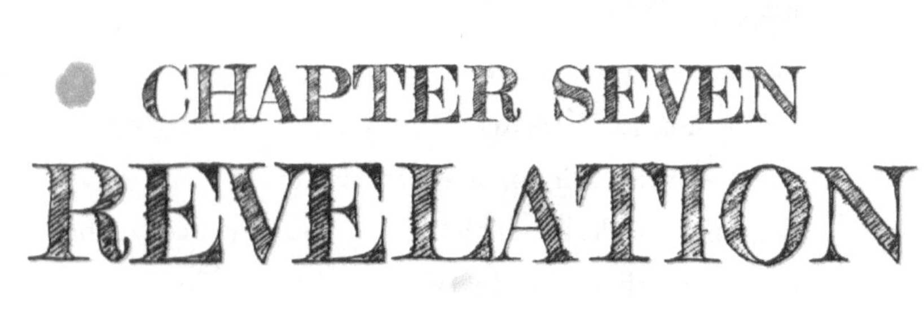

CHAPTER SEVEN
REVELATION

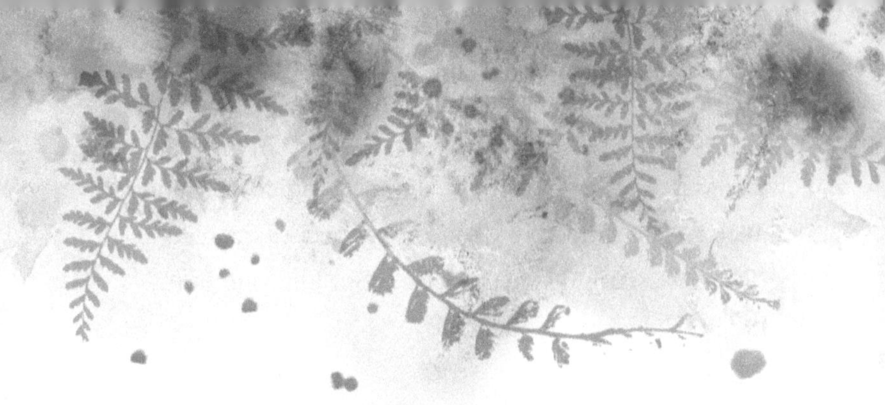

LOCATION: *NG Astraea*
28 June, Earth Year 3070
LOCAL CYCLE STATUS: *Night Six*

Around Eva, the lab hummed unevenly – power had automatically rerouted through emergency systems, lights dimmed to a sickly amber. Lina had gone on a supply run with a small group from Engineering – scavenging medical stock, portable power cells… and taking blood samples from the dead wherever they could reach them.

It'd felt like a risk letting her go – but necessary.

Eva continued her own research alone, surrounded by the quiet murmuring of the people around her.

Some sat against the walls with their knees pulled tight to their chests. Others stood rigidly, weapons clutched in white-knuckled hands, eyes fixed on the static-laced monitors and glass walls as if looking away invited a death sentence.

There was nothing she could do about Lina out there.

So Eva did what she could.

She worked.

For hours she sifted through research logs, medical records, and environmental scans, chasing patterns through the *Astraea's* failing databases. When her eyes finally began to burn from the screens, she pushed herself away from the console and moved through the room instead.

The laboratory had become a refuge by necessity rather than design. Word had obviously spread that survivors were holed up here.

Eva glanced around the area. Tables, fridges, and stools had been pushed against the glass walls that separated them from the corridor in the hope of hiding them from any of the reanimated. It created a makeshift safe zone that stretched across the three inter-connected labs and a narrow storage bay. It wasn't big, but it was all they had.

She counted the survivors. There were twenty-one of them now, not including Lina and the five that had gone with her.

She crouched beside a young technician who had been shaking since Lina left, offering a few soft words and a steady hand on his shoulder until his breathing slowed. Nearby, she checked a woman's bandaged arm, tightening the wrap and murmuring reassurance she wasn't entirely sure she believed herself.

As she moved between them, she asked questions and took blood samples.

Names.

Departments.

Blood types.

Most people barely thought about the answer.

'O negative,' one technician said absently, rubbing tired eyes.

'Same here,' another replied from across the room.

Eva nodded, committing each response to memory before moving on.

Eventually, with little more she could do for them, she returned to the console.

If anyone was still moving – *and alive* – through the ship, she wanted to know.

The surveillance feeds flickered as they came online, one after another stabilising across the console.

Corridor after corridor appeared empty.

Then one feed shifted.

Eva froze.

The ghost deer had returned.

It no longer resembled the animal that had once wandered through the *Greenbelt*. Its white fur was matted dark with blood; patches of hide had been torn away entirely, exposing raw muscle and glimpses of bone beneath. The antler that had hung loose earlier was gone now – torn free completely and lodged through the side of its neck like a crude spear. The remaining antlers were twisted and broken, jutting at unnatural angles as the creature reared back and hurled itself forward at the ship.

Impact.

The wall buckled with a metallic shriek.

Several people flinched. One woman let out a strangled sob and had to be steadied by the man beside her.

Again.

And again.

The sound of bone cracking and metal warping. It echoed through the speakers, vibrating up the console and into Eva's palms.

Her breathing turned shallow.

This wasn't rage or hunger.

It was compulsion – the same dead urgency she'd seen in Commander Reyes. A host driven by invasive spores, its only remaining purpose to multiply and spread.

The deer slammed its skull into the side of the *Astraea* once more. Antlers splintered further as blood dripped on the ground in a pool of dark red.

Something inside Eva shattered with it.

The monitors smeared into streaks of light as her knees buckled. Strength vanished all at once, and she slid down to the floor, breath tearing painfully from her chest.

No one moved to touch her.

She folded in on herself, pressing her forehead to her knees, fists clenched tight in her hair. The sound of impact still rang in her ears, each blow echoing like a countdown.

Lukas' face flashed behind her eyes – his stare hollow, bleeding, screaming for help.

Then his body, twisted and ruined, head dangling by torn tendons as Commander Reyes devoured him.

Erik followed.

Steady. Warm. Smiling softly as he bent down on one knee and told her he would dedicate every moment of his life to her – to whispering his love as he stepped backwards into the void of space without hesitation.

Both of them had loved her.

Erik without a second thought for himself...

Lukas in his own sick and twisted way...

And both of them had died for that love.

Her chest tightened until she couldn't breathe.

A sound tore out of her – something between a sob and a broken laugh. She pressed her fists hard against her eyes until stars burst behind her lids.

"They come from the Lumen Fern!" Lukas' voice cut through the fog – frantic, desperate, final.

Eva sucked in a sharp breath.

Lina was kneeling in front of her now, saying her name, asking something she couldn't process. The lab blurred as Eva pushed herself upright so fast the room tilted.

'My notebook,' she said, staggering to a workbench to steady herself. She yanked the field journal from her back pocket. Pages fluttered past – careful sketches, neat annotations, soil descriptions, growth patterns – until she found it.

Polypodiophyta luminis – Lumen Fern.

Her own handwriting stared back at her.

Appears to grow on decaying biomass. Unable to identify further as the night cycle begins.

She swallowed hard.

Decaying biomass.

Her gaze slid to the specimen jar sitting atop the surveillance console. Inside, faintly luminous pink spores drifted in slow suspension, utterly indifferent.

'Lina,' Eva said, her voice trembling despite her effort to steady it. 'I think I've figured it out...'

Lina stepped closer. Her eyes were red rimmed with the lack of sleep. Several others leaned in: a hydroponics tech, an engineer with a bloodstained shirt, the medic whose hands shook from losing his last patient.

'So did I,' Lina said, shrugging off a pack from her shoulder and dropping it onto the nearby bench. Several sealed sample vials clinked together inside.

'Blood samples,' Lina said, breath uneven. 'From the corridors. From the ones who didn't make it.'

Eva stepped closer. 'You tested them?'

'On the way back. Quick scans only – but enough. Not one of them was O negative.'

Eva nodded towards the room. 'I checked everyone here too. Our theory's correct – all O neg.'

She exhaled slowly, dragging a hand down her face before turning to them.

'Listen to me,' she said, voice hoarse but steady. 'All of you.'

The room quieted, even the ones on the edge of panic turned.

'We're not just surviving by chance,' Eva continued. 'There's a reason we're still here.'

She gestured towards Lina, then to the samples.

'We think it's our blood type. Everyone here is O negative, that might be why it's not taking hold in us.'

'But that doesn't make us safe,' Lina added quickly. 'It just means we have time.'

Eva turned, grabbing the interactive board and pulling it towards her. She exhaled slowly and continued. 'Spores are reproductive. They disperse, germinate, and regrow.'

She gestured to the jar. 'But these evolved differently. They thrive on living biomass.'

She began writing, showing everyone that had gathered around the connections she had made.

'They infect a host and interface with the brain stem,' Eva said, sketching a crude stick figure. 'The body breaks down and the spores draw on what's left – heat, nutrients – until the host dies.'

She drew small dots representing spores invading the figure and an arrow pointing to a hastily drawn skull – meant to signify death.

'They reanimate the host then, just long enough to spread further.' She swallowed as she forced the next part out. 'But the host isn't what infects you. Not directly.' Her gaze flicked to the jar again, then back to the others. 'The spores are.'

She hesitated, her thoughts racing, adjusting to what she now understood.

'The spores can permeate the skin, settle, and grow...' Her voice tightened. 'The attacks aren't the infection. They're the delivery system.'

She looked up, meeting their eyes as a murmur of confusion rippled through the room.

'It's not hunger,' Eva said quickly, shaking her head. 'Not in any human sense. It's propagation. The brain stem is still functioning, but it's being overridden – reduced to our more primitive bases.' She exhaled shakily.

'So... the people?' someone from the back of the room asked. 'They—are they still *in* there?'

Eva shook her head. 'No,' she said quietly. 'Once the spores take hold of the brain stem... they stop being who they were.'

The room remained silent, but Eva carried on.

'When they attack – when they break the skin – they force a transfer of spores. It overwhelms the body before it has any chance to resist.' Her voice dropped to add, 'Even if we survive the spore transfer, we're still at risk of blood loss from their *violent tendencies.*'

Silence fell heavy over the room.

No one moved. Somewhere in the ship a metal panel creaked, followed by a distant, hollow thud that made several people flinch. One of the technicians quietly pulled a tissue from their sleeve and began to weep. Another muttered a prayer.

'But I have a theory,' Eva continued quietly. 'Once dawn comes, the spores *should* deteriorate.'

'*Should* deteriorate?' the medic asked shakily. 'What does that even mean? How do you know?'

Eva hesitated. 'I don't,' she said at last. 'I mean – not for certain.'

A ripple of unease passed through the room.

She forced herself to keep going.

'But everything I've researched so far points to a photoreactive cycle,' she said, turning back to the console, pulling up environmental logs and growth data with shaking hands. 'The fern itself thrives during the daylight window, but during nightfall, it stopped metabolising and released these spores instead.'

She highlighted the readings, numbers almost blurring together.

'The spores themselves don't photosynthesise,' Eva said. 'They're metabolically active only during temperature collapse and light absence. Once the sun rises and temperatures stabilise again, the spores *should* degrade, break down, and disappear.'

Should.

She exhaled slowly as the room remained silent.

'But,' she added quietly, because she owed them honesty, 'this species evolved here. It's alien, and it's obviously nothing like the samples from Earth I've studied.' Her fingers curled against the edge of the console. 'If it's adapted further than I think – if it can persist past dawn – then everything changes.'

Lina jumped in. 'So we wait—'

A sound interrupted her.

A weak, irregular thud against the laboratory door.

Everyone turned.

At first, Eva thought it was another one of the infected. She grabbed her gun, ready to defend.

Then she heard it.

'Please,' a small voice whimpered. 'Please... someone help me... it hurts.'

Lina and Eva moved together towards the door.

A teenager stood outside the sealed glass – a girl no older than sixteen or seventeen. Her whole life before her.

Her hair was plastered to her forehead with sweat. Her eyes were glassy, unfocused. Blood streamed freely from her nose, and her hands left smeared prints as she pounded weakly on the door.

'Make it stop,' the girl sobbed. 'I don't want to hurt anyone.'

Eva's heart tore when she saw the bite mark on her lower arm.

'No,' she whispered instinctively. 'No, I can't—'

The girl slid down the door as her legs gave out. Her breathing hitched, then fractured into panicked gasps.

'I don't—want to turn—into a... monster,' she whispered. 'Please—help me...'

Lina covered her mouth, tears spilling freely now.

'Eva,' she said softly. 'She's not going to make it.'

'She's—she's just a kid,' someone else whispered behind them.

The girl's eyes rolled back as a low, strangled sound clawed its way out of her throat.

Eva stared down at the gun she still held in her hand.

The girl lay just outside the door, breath coming in shallow, broken pulls. Her fists now limp as her blood smeared the door.

I can't, Eva thought, her hands trembling.

And then Erik was there – not as he'd died, but as he'd lived.

Sitting beside her on the edge of the training deck, boots dangling over open space, the hum of the ship steady beneath them. He'd been cleaning his handgun after practise, movements slow, deliberate.

She'd asked him how he could do it – how he could walk into danger knowing he might not come back.

He'd looked at her then, surprised. 'Because if we don't protect our people,' he'd said gently, 'we stop being human.'

Erik had smiled – soft, sad, and brave all at once.

The memory dissolved.

Eva swallowed hard.

This wasn't about murder. This was about refusing to let a child lose herself to something cruel and alien and irreversible.

I'm not killing her, Eva told herself, heart breaking open in her chest. *I'm keeping her humanity alive.*

She stepped forward as she opened the door seal.

The girl looked up at her, tears streaking her cheeks.

'I'm scared,' she breathed faintly. 'I want my dad. Do you know where he is?'

Eva knelt, tears falling unchecked as she brushed strands of hair back from the girl's face.

'I know, sweetheart,' she whispered. 'It's going to be okay. He'll be with you very soon.'

The lie tasted bitter, but it was kinder than the truth.

She pressed the barrel gently to the girl's forehead, and without hesitation, pulled the trigger.

The sound thundered. Several people screamed. Someone retched. Lina immediately leaped forward to embrace Eva.

The girl crumpled instantly.

For a single, fragile moment, nothing happened.

Then her body jerked.

A wet, choking sound tore from her throat as her limbs spasmed against the floor.

Eva froze.

'No...'

Beneath the torn bite mark on the girl's arm, something shifted. A faint, unnatural bulge – like something pressing outward from within.

The flesh split, oozing dark liquid in slow drips that pooled beneath her.

Lina gasped.

Thin, pale fronds pushed through the wound, slick with blood, unfurling in trembling, instinctive curls. A faint pink glow pulsed at their tips.

More followed.

Along her neck. Her collarbone. Beneath the skin of her cheek, something writhed before tearing free in a delicate, blooming rupture.

Someone screamed.

The girl's body arched violently – then collapsed back against the floor as the growth spread in rapid, silent bursts, drinking in what remained.

Eva's stomach dropped.

She'd seen this before on Reyes.

The fronds twitched once... then stilled.

Silence fell over the lab.

Eva didn't remember standing up, but at some point she must have moved – lifting the teen gently from the floor, carrying her through the lab doors. The motion felt automatic, distant, like her body knew what to do even as her mind fractured behind it.

The others parted without a word.

Hands reached for her – steadying, supportive – but she barely felt them. Someone took the weapon from her slack fingers. Someone else wrapped a thermal blanket around the girl's small, still form, as they respectfully placed her on a table and draped a sheet over her.

There was nowhere to bury her. Eva didn't even know her name.

Eva sat on the floor with her back against the wall, staring at nothing.

The hum of the *Astraea* pressed in around her – strained, uneven, wounded. For the first time, she noticed how old the ship felt. How tired. Eight centuries of carrying hope through vacuum, and now bleeding out in the darkness of this alien world.

"If we don't protect our people..." Erik's voice came quietly this time – not sharp with memory, not soaked in grief. As if he was telling her it was okay. "*... we stop being human."*

Eva closed her eyes.

This wasn't about science anymore. Not entirely.

Understanding the fern wouldn't have saved the young girl. Knowledge alone wasn't enough – it never had been.

When she finally looked up, the people around her were watching – not with fear, not with judgment, but with something heavier. Recognition.

They knew what she'd done.

And they knew she'd done it for the girl – and for them.

Eva pushed herself to her feet, legs unsteady but holding. Lina was there instantly, arms around her, grounding her always.

'We can't stay,' Lina said quietly. 'Even if we follow the sunlight. Even if we run.'

'This world isn't safe,' someone else said. 'And neither is the *Astraea* anymore.'

Eva glimpsed back once more at the monitors – at the dead that moved and the spores that fed on death.

Then she turned back to the people. *Her* people.

'We leave,' she said. 'We find a way off this damned planet.'

CHAPTER EIGHT
UNVEILED

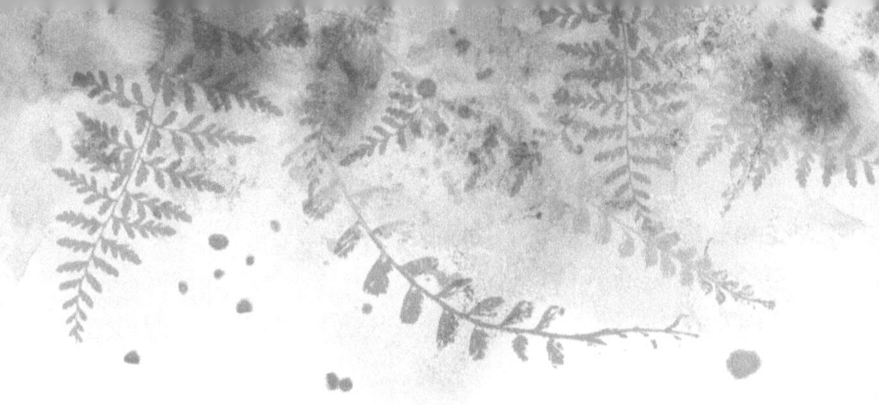

LOCATION: *NG Astraea*

29 June, Earth Year 3070

LOCAL CYCLE STATUS: *Twenty-eight hours until dawn*

The *Astraea* no longer felt like home. It felt like a coffin – the same kind they had sealed for Erik, cold and empty, drifting into the endless dark.

Emergency lighting cast long, uneven shadows through the lab as people moved with quiet urgency, voices low, movements clipped. The hum of life support systems was uneven now – a strained, laboured rhythm that reminded Eva of a failing heart-beat.

They were preparing to leave.

Not evacuate – the word had been quietly abandoned – but to find a way to somehow keep the *Astraea* alive. Stabilise her systems or find a safe area to regroup – some ground that wouldn't kill them before dawn.

Survivors clustered in tense pockets, sorting supplies scavenged from medical hubs and emergency lockers. Ammunition was counted, then counted again, and weapons were checked with trembling hands before being gripped a little too tightly.

Near the far wall, a mother crouched with her child pressed tightly to her chest, one hand clamped protectively over the back of his head.

Some spoke in whispers about the dead – how many they would meet in the corridors, how many might still be stalking in the shadows.

No one raised their voice or argued. No one needed to.

Eva moved among them like a ghost, her boots barely registering on the polished floor. She responded when spoken to, nodded when plans were outlined, but her mind remained half a step removed – ticking through variables, replaying images from the monitors, replaying the soft final sound of the gunshot that had ended the girl's suffering.

Eva didn't let herself dwell on it. She couldn't.

At the edge of the surveillance console, she stopped.

The interface still pulsed faintly, dim but functional. A single notification blinked at the bottom of the screen – the data log from Command she'd forwarded earlier – forgotten until now.

She tapped it open.

A priority message bloomed on the display.

NG *HERMES* – PENDING NG COMMAND ACCESS ONLY.

Lina stepped up beside her. 'We need to see this,' she said, already pulling a chair towards a monitor. 'There might be something here, Eva. Something that might help us.'

Eva nodded and slid into the adjacent seat. The bloodstained access card from Commander Reyes was still in her pocket. She drew it out and swiped it, fingers moving on instinct as the system accepted the credentials.

The message expanded in front of her, lines of encrypted data resolving slowly as the system struggled to compensate for the loss of minor network connections.

She skimmed the timestamp first.

Message Received: 18 May, Earth Year 3070.

Estimated Arrival to HDX-2719 system: 7.4 months.

Her breath left her in a slow, hollow exhale.

The Hermes.

Another *New Generation* colony ship launched after the *Astraea*.

Earth hadn't had the resources to send all ships out at the same time. They'd each been built, fuelled, and launched whenever they were ready, timed to narrow orbital windows that couldn't be missed.

They'd all been scattered into the dark like that.

Separate and alone.

Rescue was coming – but it was seven months away.

Too long. Too late.

Even if they survived the nights, even if dawn offered some fragile reprieve, the *Hermes* was still far out in the void – another fragile pocket of humanity, blind to what waited here.

Eva closed the log.

The *Astraea* was failing faster now. Key systems were in critical condition, and there were no longer enough people alive to maintain them. The ship had never been designed to run without humans.

It had an AI system on board – every *New Generation* vessel did.

But it wasn't built to think.

It was only a caretaker. Designed by the last engineers on Earth to follow human instructions, maintain technical balance, and preserve what already existed – not to adapt, not to learn, not to survive if something new occurred.

Eva stared at a readout of the failing diagnostics, watching error loops repeat, systems cycling through protocols that no longer applied.

The AI wasn't helping at all, only maintaining a version of the ship that no longer existed without human intervention.

Her jaw tightened.

Someone had made that decision long before *Astraea* ever left Earth. To keep control in human hands.

Now there were barely any humans left.

And the system built to protect them was now obsolete.

They were on their own.

'Eva.'

Lina braced herself against the console. Her dark frizzly curls were pulled back haphazardly, eyes bright with fear – the look of someone who had uncovered something they wished they hadn't.

'I pulled archived mission data,' she said quietly. 'There's some stuff Command locked down.'

Eva turned. 'Anything that can help us?'

'See for yourself.'

Lina tapped at the keyboard. Overlapping orbital schematics filled the display – and Eva's stomach dropped.

Two planetary tracks.

One highlighted in pale green.

One in warning amber.

'This,' Lina said, tapping the green arc, 'is the original target. HDX-2719-c. *Planet C.* The one Earth cleared for colonisation.'

Eva leaned closer. 'Yes, that's where we are.'

'Nope. Look again,' Lina pointed to the second track – the amber one. 'That's where we are. *Planet B.*'

It sat just inside the first, its orbital period shorter, and inclination subtly different.

'Eva – we're on the wrong fucking planet.'

Eva's pulse quickened as she noticed the positional overlay.

'That doesn't make sense. With all the sensors on this ship? Orbital telemetry, stellar positioning, deep scans – there's no way they'd confuse two planets in the same system.'

Lina dragged a hand over her face. 'Unless they couldn't see it properly.'

Eva stared at the orbital tracks.

'Remember Reyes explained that solar radiation blinded half the instruments,' Lina murmured. 'If *Planet C* was directly behind the sun during approach—'

Eva's stomach twisted. '—they must've thought they were the same body,' she whispered.

'Or close enough not to matter,' Lina said. 'Atmospheric stability. Water. Magnetosphere. Biological markers.'

Eva straightened, cold spreading through her chest. 'Is there anything else?'

Lina's mouth tightened. 'There's a log from Commander Reyes.' Lina's mouth tightened. 'I haven't watched it yet...' She tapped a button and the screen juddered, then stabilised.

Reyes appeared, seated at the console. Her uniform was immaculate, posture rigid, her hair set into a stiff bun, the way Eva remembered – nothing like the blood-soaked creature she'd faced hours earlier.

The timestamp glowed in the corner of the frame.

COMMAND LOG – REYES, MARLINA

25 June, Earth Year 3070 – 10 Earth days post landing

'Begin log.'

Reyes glanced briefly off screen before continuing. 'Orbital recalibration complete. Planetary mass, axial tilt, and atmospheric composition fall within acceptable variance.' A pause. 'However... our position has revealed an issue.'

Her fingers tapped once against the desk.

'Solar activity upon entry into the HDX-2719 system exceeded projections. Because of this, key operating systems within the *Astraea* were severely compromised, and we had to rely on orbital mapping generated eight centuries ago.'

Her jaw tightened. 'Simply put: we've landed on the wrong planet.'

She hesitated as a shout echoed from somewhere behind her, but carried on.

'Comparative analysis is ongoing, but scans indicate discrepancies between the planetary body we've landed on and the original survey data. Our designated landing target – HDX-2719-c, otherwise known as *Planet C* – appears to have emerged from stellar occultation.'

She leaned closer to the camera now, voice lowering.

'There's been a grave error. If we'd waited just a little longer, we would've seen *Planet C* emerge from behind the sun, and we wouldn't be in this position.'

She straightened, professionalism snapping back into place.

'We're on HDX-2719-b. A secondary body previously dismissed as marginally habitable due to its proximity to the star.' She glanced down at unseen data. 'While our initial investigations deemed this place as capable of sustaining human life, the night cycle exceeds projections. Native flora activity is… unusually active.'

A faint sound carried through the recording again – raised voices, indistinct but angry.

'Several members of Command have expressed the desire to relaunch during the next orbital window.' Her tone hardened. 'Those concerns are… unrealistic.'

She folded her hands together.

'The *Astraea* was designed to anchor. We simply don't have the resources to construct a launch cradle at this time. Attempting ascent now would tear the hull apart.'

Another sound followed – wet, dragging – but Reyes didn't appear to notice.

'We are here,' Reyes said firmly. 'And we *will* survive here. We have no other option. NG Hermes is still over seven months away, and we can seek rescue then.'

Something moved faintly in the far corner of the room, just on the edge of the frame.

'There are also reports of a spreading sickness aboard the ship. Until environmental vectors are understood, I have ordered non-essential personnel confined to the aft sectors for their protection.'

She leaned closer to the camera.

'I have reason to believe a containment seal had been compromised,' she said quietly. 'We are investigating.'

When she spoke again, her voice had softened – not with doubt, but with regret. 'If this log is being reviewed after the fact, then I have already been judged.'

She reached forward, fingers brushing the console. 'We didn't land here because of malice, ambition, or negligence.'

Her eyes lifted to the camera one last time.

'We landed here simply because we believed the Earth data. We—I did my best, but now I fear I have just committed over five thousand souls to their graves.'

The shadow moved closer behind her, emitting a low growl.

Reyes frowned slightly.

Slowly, she turned.

Eva recognised him as Second Class Daniel Clark – part of Erik's unit. He stood, swaying gently just a few metres behind her.

'Clark, wha—what are you doing?' Reyes stuttered.

He stepped forward into the light.

His lower jaw hung loose, torn almost completely free. Blood slicked his uniform collar, black and drying in thick ropes down his chest. Something pale twitched in the shredded muscle of his throat.

Another low growl crawled out of what remained of his mouth.

Reyes rose halfway from her chair.

'Daniel! Are you okay? We need to get you some help! Wha—'

The camera jolted as Reyes slammed backward into the console. His ruined mouth crashed against her shoulder, teeth punching through skin with a wet crack.

She screamed.

Blood erupted across the screen in a violent arc, splattering the lens as Daniels tore into her. The recording captured only fragments after that – her hands clawing at his face, his fingers digging into her uniform, the choking gurgle of his throat filling with her blood.

The console overturned.

The camera toppled sideways.

For a moment the floor filled the frame as Reyes fled the room, one hand pressed to her bleeding shoulder while Clark dragged himself after her, the wet scrape of his body fading as the feed dissolved into static.

Eva stared at the frozen screen.

She thought of the Lumen Fern, glowing gently under the daylight. Thought of how harmless it had seemed.

We never stood a chance.

A sharp clang echoed down the corridor. Someone swore under their breath.

'We have to warn the Hermes,' Lina said suddenly. 'Before they make the same mistake.'

Eva nodded, resolve snapping into place.

Lina was already pulling up schematics, fingers flying. 'Flight control would be best for that. Direct access to long range comms.'

Behind them, someone laughed – a short, fractured sound.

'Did you not just watch the same log we did?' a man said hoarsely. 'This ship isn't going anywhere.'

'Then what the hell are we doing?' another voice cut in, sharp with rising panic. 'Sitting here until we die?'

The room began to fracture – overlapping arguments, fear bleeding into anger.

Eva glanced around the lab.

For hours these people had moved like parts of the same failing machine – packing ammunition, tending wounds with the last of the medkits, and standing watch over the corridor outside while others rested. No one had really known each other before tonight, but fear and necessity had forced them into something resembling a team.

Now that fragile rhythm was breaking apart.

The cohesion they'd held together with plans and motion was unravelling now that the truth had stripped them bare.

Before Eva could speak—

A thud. Wet. Heavy.

The corridor lights flickered.

Then the unmistakable sound of too many feet moving in unison.

Lina's face drained of colour. 'That's... that's not just one of them.'

The door at the far end of the room began to bow inward, metal screaming as something on the other side pressed against it with inhuman force.

A hand slapped uselessly against the glass – skin greyed, fingers bent at the wrong angles. Then another. And another.

The glass began to crack under the pressure.

'Move,' Eva said, voice cutting through the paralysis. 'Now!'

The door gave way.

Bodies spilled through – bloodied, twisted and jerking, eyes vacant and mouths opened in soundless snarls.

The first wave tore into the nearest cluster of fleeing crew at the opposite end of the lab, dragging them down into the floor in a collapsing knot of limbs and screams. Gunfire erupted somewhere to the left, sharp and panicked, but it barely slowed them.

A man made it three steps before something hit him from behind. He went down hard and didn't get back up.

Screams and gunfire filled the lab as people broke in different directions, splitting the room into pockets of chaos.

Eva grabbed Lina's wrist and ran, screaming for the others to follow. Boots skidded across the floor as the dead surged forward, relentless and tireless. She saw people fall – dragged beneath grasping hands, teeth tearing, flesh ripping – their screams cutting off one by one beneath the growling chorus.

'This way!' someone shouted.

But there was nowhere to go.

The quarantine lockdown slammed through Eva's mind in a cold rush of understanding. When she and Lina had sealed the labs, the system had locked every external door in the sector – leaving only maintenance access routes and service infrastructure free.

More bodies pushed through the broken doorway, piling over one another in a writhing mass. Gunfire cracked again, but the sound was swallowed by the relentless groaning of the infected flooding the room.

Eva spun in place, heart hammering, searching—

Erik's smile flashed through her mind.

"I love you..."

That's when she saw it.

A maintenance hatch.

'Ventilation shaft!' Eva shouted, pointing to the ceiling.

A desk had been shoved beneath it, metal legs screeching across the floor. One by one, survivors hauled themselves up, hands gripping edges, boots slipping as the room beneath them collapsed into chaos.

At the edge of the room, the reanimated shifted – drawn by movement, by sound, by the last pockets of humanity still struggling at the back of the lab.

Lina went first, hauled up by two shaking hands. Eva followed, pushing others ahead of her, before pulling herself into the shaft last.

A set of snapping teeth caught at her boot as she kicked free.

The hatch slammed shut.

Something heavy struck it immediately from below.

Then again.

They didn't stop.

'Go, just go!' Eva whispered urgently, as they crawled blindly through the dark.

The screams and growls began to fade behind them, replaced by the echoing thrum of the *Astraea's* failing systems.

Around them, the ship was dying.

And ahead—

No plan.

No one to save them.

No dawn yet in sight.

Only the dark.

CHAPTER NINE
COUNTDOWN

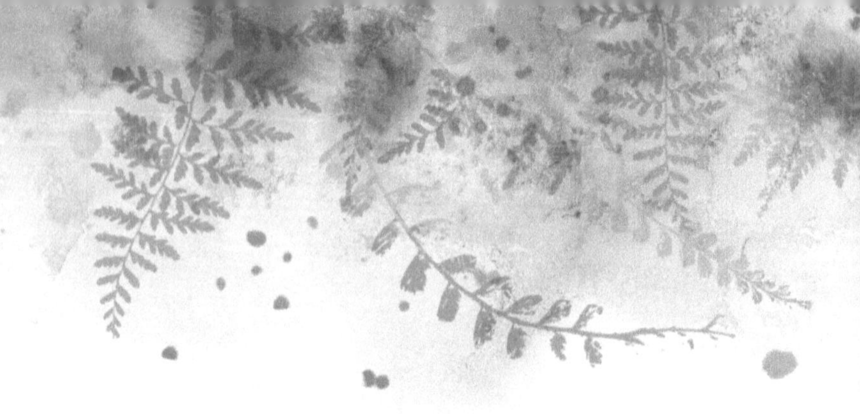

LOCATION: *NG Astraea*

30 June, Earth Year 3070

LOCAL CYCLE STATUS: *Three hours until dawn*

The ventilation shafts twisted and narrowed the deeper they crawled, their metal walls slick with condensation and centuries of dust buildup. The air grew warmer, thicker – stale with the lingering copper tang of blood that seemed baked into the ship.

They crawled in silence.

Eva led where she could, driven only by the instinct to put distance between them and the sound of growling. Behind her, Lina moved with grim determination, guiding others through tight bends and vertical drops. There were eighteen of them left now – those who had made it into the vents before the infected had descended on them all.

Eva caught brief glimpses of them in the narrow crawlspace as they moved – Ashwin from hydroponics dragging a bruised leg behind him, a young medic named Amara clutching the last of the field bandages to her chest, two silent security officers bringing up the rear with their rifles pressed tight to the metal walls.

Fewer voices than before. Fewer heartbeats.

But still alive.

Still my people.

After a long stretch – long enough that Eva's arms trembled and her lungs burned – the sounds finally faded. Only the low drone of the ship remained, faltering and uneven, resonating through the walls.

Eva slowed to listen, raising a fist to signal the others to stop.

'I think it's clear,' she whispered.

They shifted to the end of the shaft and dropped through a maintenance grate one by one, landing in a dim service corridor. Emergency lights flickered overhead, illuminating glowing signage half obscured by dark smears Eva pretended not to see.

COMMONS HUB

'Food hall,' Lina murmured.

They moved carefully, weapons raised, every step measured. The corridor opened into a wide chamber – and for a moment, no one breathed.

The hall was vast, its ceiling arched and ribbed with support beams. Long circular tables stood abandoned, trays and utensils scattered where meals had been interrupted mid-bite. Reinforced viewing windows stretched from floor to ceiling along the far wall, offering an uninterrupted view of the *Aurelion Basin* beyond.

For a heartbeat, Eva didn't see the ruin within.

She saw the three of them instead – herself, Erik, and Lina crammed around one of the tables after a long shift, boots kicked out, sleeves rolled up. Erik had been halfway through explaining a flight manoeuvre with a fork, tracing imaginary trajectories through the air, while Lina barely pretended to listen. Her attention had been fixed on the open kitchen, chin propped in her hands, trying – and failing – to be subtle as she made eyes at one of the chefs.

The chef had noticed. He'd grinned, exaggeratedly wiping down the counter just to make Lina laugh.

Eva remembered thinking, absurdly, that this place felt alive then.

Outside, the world was changing.

The horizon glowed with a deep, bruised red. Dawn was creeping steadily over the land like a slow bleed. The light was harsh, almost viscous, staining the clouds and terrain as if the planet itself was wounded.

Someone behind Eva let out a quiet, broken sound.

'Is that... daylight?' a man whispered.

'Almost,' Eva said. 'Three, maybe four hours. Give or take.'

Three hours until the spores either die – or don't.

The hall itself was empty.

No bodies. No movement. No signs of struggle beyond the abandoned meals.

They swept the space in small groups. The kitchen doors sat to one side of the hall – heavy, industrial, sealed tight. Cold storage units hummed faintly beyond them.

That's when they heard it.

Knock.

Knock.

Knock.

Every weapon came up at once.

'It's a trick,' someone hissed. 'They're learning!'

Eva raised a hand, forcing stillness. Her pulse hammered, but something about the sound scraped against her instincts – not frantic, not animal.

Human.

She stepped closer to the door, boots echoing too loudly in the cavernous space. 'Is anyone in there?'

Then, hesitant and trembling—

'Please,' a voice called through the metal. 'Help... We're alive. We're not infected.'

Lina sucked in a sharp breath. 'I recognise that voice. That's—that's my aunt!'

Eva turned. Lina's face had gone pale, eyes wide and glassy.

'Kara?' Lina called. 'Aunty Kara, it's me. Lina!'

There was a sharp inhale on the other side, followed by a muffled voice saying, 'Get out of my damn way!'

Eva pulled the door open.

Faces stared back at them – drawn tight with hunger and fear, eyes hollowed by sleeplessness. Some clutched knives, broken chair legs, scavenged tools. Others held onto each other like they might vanish if they let go. They smelled of sweat, stale air, and desperation.

But they were alive.

A woman surged forward and wrapped Lina in a fierce embrace.

'I thought you were dead,' she cried, fingers digging into Lina's jacket. 'I searched everywhere—I thought—'

'I'm here, Aunty Kara,' Lina whispered, tears spilling freely now as she clung to her. 'I'm here.'

Eva watched them, chest tightening as she saw the relief flood Lina's face after everything she'd endured.

She knew enough to understand Lina's pain. Her mother had died slowly, cancer eating her from the inside out. Her father hadn't lasted long after either – a sudden heart attack. The doctors had called it stress-induced cardiomyopathy.

Broken heart syndrome.

Her aunt Kara had stepped in after that. Filled the gap her parents had left broken and empty.

It was why she and Eva had chased a cure, and they'd found it – too late for her mother – but named it for her anyway.

Carina.

A final act of a daughter's love – carved into science.

'Block the main entry doors,' Eva said, eyes never leaving the small windows showing the corridor beyond the hall.

One of the engineers who had survived the lab with them nodded and moved immediately, dragging a table across the threshold while others reinforced it with storage racks and freezer trolleys.

Once the doors were secured, Eva turned back to the group.

She didn't soften the truth – there was no point.

She told them about the spores, and the infection.

About the wrong planet. That the real *Planet C* was still out there, untouched, orbiting patiently beyond the sun.

And finally, about the rescue that wouldn't come for over half an Earth year.

Faces drained of colour as reality settled in.

'So you're saying,' one woman murmured, 'this was all a mistake?'

'Yes, in more ways than one,' Eva said quietly. 'And we're all paying for it.'

A man in a pilot's uniform stepped forward. His name patch was scorched, the fabric stiff with dried blood, his eyes rimmed red from exhaustion.

'New Generation Defence, Third Class,' he said. 'Name's Nate. Nate Cowan.'

Eva nodded in acknowledgment. Her gaze caught on the insignia stitched into his sleeve – battalion markings.

First Class Defence officers like Erik had overseen everything. There were six captains in total, each responsible for one of six defence divisions, coordinating strategic control, threat response, and ship security. Erik had been one of those six.

Second Class formed the backbone – flight control, weapons systems, and critical infrastructure – each assigned to a squadron under a First Class leader.

Third Class filled the gaps. Peacekeepers. First responders. The ones who dealt with problems before they ever reached Command.

The insignia on Nate's arm matched Erik's squad. Eva would recognise it anywhere. First Class leaders were permitted to choose their own insignia upon promotion.

Her throat tightened.

A green leaf.

He'd chosen it for her.

Eva forced the thought away.

'Once a ship like this lands, it isn't meant to lift again,' Nate continued. 'The *Astraea's* engines aren't designed for planetary ascent — not without a cradle, years of construction, and resources we don't have.'

'I know,' Eva said. 'Commander Reyes confirmed all of that.'

A ripple of murmurs passed through the room.

'Then what's the plan?' someone snapped. 'Just wait here until we turn into—into them?'

Nate hesitated. 'Well, there are the escape pods.'

The room hushed.

'They're designed for orbital evacuation,' he continued quickly. 'Short range. Limited life support. But they can clear the atmosphere. If we reach orbit, we could redirect – slingshot towards *Planet C*. Maybe even establish comms with the NG Hermes once they reach the system.'

Eva's mind was already running trajectories. Failure points. Margins of error.

Things she had never imagined thinking about as an astrobotanist.

'They've got basic supplies too,' Nate added, almost as an afterthought. 'Rations, water recyclers... enough to keep us alive while we wait.'

'How many can they carry?'

'Everyone here, easily,' Nate said. Then grimaced. 'Getting to them is the problem.'

'Why?' Lina asked.

Nate exhaled. 'They're at the back of the ship. Well past the labs.'

'That's where you just came from, right? The labs?' someone said.

'Yes,' Eva replied. 'And there's a whole horde down there.' She folded her arms. 'We can't draw them away. There's simply too many.' Her jaw tightened. 'And I won't sacrifice anyone to try otherwise.'

There's been enough death already.

Before Nate could speak, the floor shuddered.

Not a violent jolt – something deeper. A long, resonant tremor rolled through the walls as the pale amber lights overhead flickered.

Once.

Twice.

Then steadied – but dimmer than before.

A sharp tone cut through the air.

Text crawled across the nearest wall display as power rerouted.

EVACUATION PROTOCOL – ACTIVE

SECTOR LOCKDOWN INITIATED

The room went very still.

Kara frowned. 'What does that mean?'

Eva didn't answer immediately.

Across the room, Lina was staring at the screen.

Their eyes met.

A cold memory surfaced – days earlier, sealing the lab and forcing the system into a partial lockdown just to survive the first outbreak.

'Oh, shit,' Lina said under her breath.

Another vibration rippled through the deck.

Somewhere below them, a heavy clang echoed – the unmistakable sound of a bulkhead sealing.

A new warning flashed.

PRIMARY ACCESS CORRIDORS – LOCKDOWN PENDING

ESTIMATED SEAL TIME: 00:47:18

'Did we do this?' Eva asked quietly.

Nate turned to her. 'What?'

'Days ago,' she said, forcing the words out. 'When the outbreak started. We triggered a containment protocol, but the system wouldn't respond properly.'

Nate's expression shifted as understanding clicked into place. 'No, this is an evacuation protocol,' he muttered.

'Evacuation?' Kara echoed.

'It closes the ship in stages,' Nate said, already tracking the schematic. 'Outer sectors first, then inward. Forces survivors towards designated exits before final lockdown.' He glanced back at the display, jaw tightening. 'It's designed for thousands of people,' he added. 'Gives them time to move ahead of the seals.'

'Then why didn't it trigger before?' Lina called out.

'Because the ship is failing,' he said. 'Or...' His gaze flicked to the warning display. 'Or your quarantine flagged the breach days ago – and the AIs only just now caught up enough to act on it.'

Across the wall display, a schematic of the *Astraea* flickered to life. Sections of the ship glowed amber as containment protocols began stepping inward, corridor by corridor.

Eva scanned it quickly.

To get to the escape pods they would have to run straight through the *Astraea's* central transit column, a long arterial corridor that cut the vessel from stern to bow.

Some sections were already beginning to seal.

'If we take the spine, we can make it before the lockdown reaches it,' Eva said quickly.

Nate swore under his breath. 'Then we run.'

Another distant clang reverberated through the hull.

Closer.

The *Astraea* was doing exactly what it had been built to do.

Just far too late.

'We move,' Eva snapped. 'Now. Everyone—go!'

They made their way through narrow service corridors, down ladders slick with condensation and blood, into shafts that smelled of oil and cold metal. Emergency lighting painted everything in flickering reds and ambers.

Along the way, Eva found more survivors.

Another medic barricaded inside a supply closet sheltering with two children. A pair of hydroponics technicians clinging to a maintenance gantry and a defence officer bleeding from a cut to the forehead.

Each time, Eva made the call quickly. 'Bring them and move!'

The ship groaned as they descended into the lower decks, doors slamming shut all around them.

Then they reached the escape pod access deck and stopped.

The corridor ahead was filled.

Not dozens.

Not hundreds.

Thousands.

Bodies packed shoulder to shoulder, swaying gently in the dim emergency lights that bled through distant observation ports. Blood-smeared skin, torn uniforms, along with a faint haze of glowing pink spores drifting through the air around them like embers, thickest where bodies sagged or split.

Eyes vacant and mouths slack.

Eva's breath caught.

The aft sectors.

Reyes' voice echoed in her mind.

"Non-essential personnel confined."

The colonists Reyes had locked away in the hope of protecting them.

Three thousand bodies stood between them and the escape pods... a sea of inhumanity.

CHAPTER TEN
DAWN

LOCATION: *NG Astraea*
1 July, Earth Year 3070
LOCAL CYCLE STATUS: *Dawn*

The reanimated stood between them and the escape pods, swaying gently as the emergency lights flickered overhead. Some leaned against the walls as though resting. Others hung slack, heads tilted at impossible angles. Torn uniforms fluttered faintly in the recycled air.

No one spoke or breathed for fear of disturbing them.

Eva felt the truth settle into her bones with brutal clarity.

We aren't getting through that.

'Back,' she whispered immediately. 'We have to go back. Now.'

Someone sobbed – a thin, breaking sound that fractured almost immediately into silence as someone else clamped a hand over their mouth.

Nate hesitated, eyes locked on the sea of bodies. 'There *might* be another way in. To the pods. But it's—'

Eva turned to him. 'Where?'

He swallowed. 'There's an exterior access airlock. It's only reachable from outside the ship.' His jaw tightened. 'Which means going outside – into the *Basin*.'

A ripple of fear passed through the group.

'And how do you expect us to launch them?' Lina cut in, voice tight. 'These pods are built for vacuum, not atmospheric ascent.'

Nate shook his head quickly. 'They're not meant to, no, but they can. Emergency thrust is enough to clear the surface if we launch from outside the hull. It'll be rough. No guidance, no proper burn sequence… but once we're clear of the atmosphere, the nav systems should stabilise.'

'That still doesn't get us out of the escape bay,' someone said.

Nate shook his head. 'The pods have manual overrides. They're mounted on launch rails – designed to eject them clear of the hull even if the primary systems fail.'

He glanced back towards the corridor, jaw tight. 'If we can access them from the outside, we can trigger the release and send them out of the airlock manually.'

Eva closed her eyes for a second.

Airlock.

The word dragged something old and sharp from her chest.

Erik, standing before her, fitting her helmet on with careful hands.

The hiss of decompression as oxygen flowed into her suit.

His hand on her shoulder, his voice steady as he whispered to her.

"I love you..."

The memory still shattered her, but beneath the pain was now something clearer. Understanding.

He had done what he had to do so she could keep living.

Eva opened her eyes.

'We go forwards,' she said. 'To the front of the ship.'

They all stared at her.

'You all know it,' she continued, voice steady despite the nausea rising within her as she nodded to the horde. 'We won't make it through that. This is the only way.'

For a moment, no one moved.

Then someone nodded.

Then another.

A woman stepped forwards, eyes red rimmed. 'You kept us alive this long,' she said quietly. 'If anyone can get us there – it's you.'

A murmur of agreement followed. Gratitude. Trust. Fear – all braided together.

Eva's throat tightened.

She turned to Lina, saying softly, 'I don't know how many of us will survive this.'

'We can do this,' Lina said as she stepped closer, pressing her forehead to Eva's. 'Remember, EH + AM – best friends forever.'

Eva let out a shaky breath. 'No matter what happens—'

'This life or the next,' Lina finished, gripping her hands. 'You're stuck with me.'

Eva smiled through the tears. 'Deal.'

A shrill alarm cut through the moment.

Nate glanced at his wrist display, face draining of colour. 'The lockdown just escalated. We've got twenty-five minutes before the forward sectors seal completely.'

Lina spun, voice cracking like a whip. 'You heard him! Go—people, now!'

The *Astraea* groaned as they ran.

Bulkheads slammed down mid-sprint. A man slipped on blood as a door crushed his arm, bone snapping beneath the force. His scream cut off as grey hands burst through the narrowing gap, dragging him back. Blood pooled beneath the door, spreading in a widening stain.

Another man was pulled screaming into a side room as arms tore him apart piece by piece, his body vanishing between twitching limbs and deep, guttural growls.

Eva barely had time to register it before a woman slipped in a pool of blood and hit the ground hard, her weapon skidding from her grip. She scrambled, fingers clawing at the metal floor as someone tried to reach for her – but something dropped from the ceiling vent above.

It landed on her back with a thud as teeth sank into her neck.

'HELP—'

The scream choked into a gurgle as blood sprayed across the corridor wall in a hot arc. The thing tore her sideways, ripping flesh free, and she went limp before anyone else could reach her.

'Keep moving!' Nate shouted, dragging the man who had tried to help her back into the flow.

The reanimated surged from side corridors – and from above. A technician was lifted clean off the floor, her arm ripped free at the shoulder. Arterial spray painted the ceiling before the rest of her body disappeared into the vents, her scream cut short in a wet snap.

Just ahead, Lina fired.

The burst of gunfire cracked through the corridor – sharp, deafening in the enclosed space. One of the reanimated jerked as a round tore through its chest, staggering it, but it didn't fall.

Another shot – this time to the head.

The skull split open in a spray of bone and grey matter, the body collapsing mid-stride. But even as it dropped, spores burst from the wound in a faint, glowing cloud.

Lina ran past an open doorway—

Hands lunged out.

Bloody. Grasping.

Eva slammed into her, grabbing Lina's arm and wrenching her back with everything she had.

Eva fired as rounds punched through skulls at arm's length, bodies jerking, collapsing, piling into the doorway as she forced them back.

'Move!' she screamed. 'Go, go, go!'

The entrance doors loomed ahead. She ran, skidding to a stop at the access panel.

EVACUATION PROTOCOL ACTIVE – ACCESS DOOR RESTRICTED

The message flashed again and again as she entered her code.

DENIED – LOCKED BY COMMAND

Of course it's fucking locked.

She ripped Reyes' card from her pocket and slammed it against the reader.

Nothing.

Again.

Nothing. Not even a tone.

Behind her, a scream brought the corridor almost to a standstill.

Eva turned and near the centre of the chaos, the mother she'd seen earlier was surrounded, clutching her son tight against her chest. She was trying to stand, but the press of bodies around them closed in too fast.

'Please—!' she cried, as decaying hands seized her.

One tore the child from her arms – a small, piercing scream as the boy was dragged backwards, fingers slipping from his mother's grasp as she lunged after him.

'NO!'

She crawled, clawing across the blood-slick floor, reaching.

But she was too late.

The reanimated closed over the boy, pulling him into the mass. His scream cut off as he was buried under the writhing mass of bodies.

The mother howled – a sound so broken it barely sounded human – and threw herself after him.

Bodies collapsed over her, tearing, pulling, her screams dissolving into the same guttural chorus as the rest.

Eva could still see the mother's hand reaching—

I can't save them all.

She slammed the card against the reader.

Her grip tightened around the card. The cracked plastic sliced into her skin, splitting it open. Her blood smeared the scanner as she struck it again and again.

'Let us the fuck out of here!'

The panel buzzed weakly as the doors shuddered – then parted.

Cold air rushed in as they spilled out onto alien soil, boots skidding on loose sediment while the first blade of scarlet sunlight crested the horizon.

More than sixty survivors scrambled forwards, instinctively gathering into a tight, ragged cluster. Their breaths fogged in the air, visible along with the faint mist rising from the *Basin* floor. The terrain was jagged, dotted with low, twisted outcrops of rock and patches of crimson cacti-type plants that seemed to glimmer in the blood-tinged light.

Some clutched makeshift weapons, others leaned on each other, trembling, unsure of where to go or what to do next. They moved together, shoulders brushing, a fragile barrier of human warmth against the unknown.

And around them, closing in from every direction, were the reanimated.

From the *Greenbelt* came animals – feral, half rotted with ribs exposed, as spores drifted lazily in the air, glowing faintly as they caught the rising light.

From the ship came their people – friends, family, and co-workers alike – pouring from the front entrance in a relentless tide. Crawling. Dragging. Reaching.

'Eva!' Lina screamed. 'What do we do?'

I don't know.

I don't—

The sky burned brighter as the sun crept over the horizon.

A ghost deer, broken and bleeding, edging closer and closer to Nate, collapsed mid-step.

Then another.

And another.

Bodies fell like puppets with cut strings – humans, animals, all of them dropping into the dust as sunlight washed over the ground. Spores flared once, brilliantly – then vanished as if they had never been there at all.

Silence fell.

Thousands of corpses lay scattered across the dirt and within the *Astraea's* long shadow.

As the sun rose fully, something else began to happen.

Like Reyes in the elevator – from torn flesh and broken chests, pale green shoots emerged.

They unfurled slowly, delicately – leaves trembling as they drank in the warmth. The living now fed from the dead, and the *Basin* bloomed with quiet, terrible beauty.

Eva stood among the bodies, chest heaving, soaked in blood and dust.

Lina stepped forward and pulled her into a fierce embrace.

For a time, neither of them spoke.

'They're... stopping,' Lina whispered finally, voice unsteady. 'You were right. The spores... they're gone.'

Eva looked out across the land. The infected lay where they'd fallen, unmoving beneath the rising sun.

But the ground around them was already changing as a new forest was beginning to grow.

Eva tightened her grip around Lina, staring at the ferns rising from the dead around them – a living ring of death.

When dawn fully claimed the sky, they found the exterior access bay they were looking for.

The escape pods waited.

Before following, Eva pulled her notebook from her pocket. Its pages were crumpled, stained dark with blood. She wrote quickly, her injured hand trembling.

If you find this note, leave this world.

If you cannot leave—

She remembered Lina's words on the last day of dusk.

—follow the sun.

She continued writing.

Night isn't safe.

As she stuck it to the entry doors, she left a bloody smudge where her thumb dragged across the page.

She read it once more, then added:

We were never meant to be here.

She signed it.

—Eva

As she stared at the note, she fiddled with the gold ring on her necklace. She looked down at it, her final reminder of the love she'd had, and lost.

She'd carried his memory through every corridor, every scream, every impossible choice.

But he wasn't here anymore.

Her gaze lifted slowly to the *Astraea* – their home.

The only one they had ever known.

With trembling hands, she unclasped the chain and slipped the ring free into her palm. The light of dawn glinted off the beautiful opal, firing off in bursts of reds, blues, and deep purples as she held it.

'I love you too, Erik. I always will,' she whispered into the air.

Eva knelt to place the ring at the foot of the door, and as she stood up, she breathed in and out deeply.

'This was our home,' she said softly. 'So you stay here.'

Eva lingered for one last second, then stood, turned, and walked away.

It was time to go.

The pods launched hours later. Eva sat strapped in beside Lina and Kara as Nate guided them – and the remaining survivors – into orbit.

His hands were steady despite the horror they left behind.

For a moment, as he reached across the console, Eva noticed the leaf insignia stitched into the sleeve of his uniform again – and smiled at the memory of him.

Below them, the planet bloomed.

Entire forests of Lumen Fern spread across the region, green and radiant, drinking deeply from what humanity had left behind.

When the sensors cleared, it appeared.

HDX-2719-c.

Smaller and dimmer – a pale wash of blue, green, and white against the void.

The real Planet C.

Eva felt no awe or relief.

Only a dull, hollow grief for a world they should never have discovered – and the people who would never see another dawn.

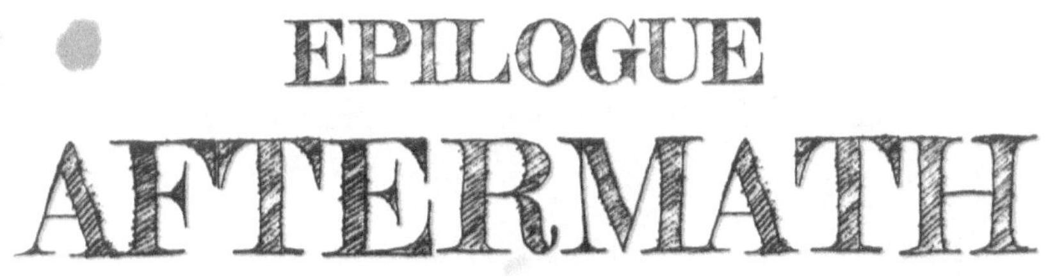
EPILOGUE
AFTERMATH

LOCATION: *NG Astraea – Emergency Beacon Site*
14 February, Earth Year 3071
LOCAL CYCLE STATUS: *Dusk Approaching*

The doors of the *Astraea* stood open.

Not a single soul remained.

Erik Calder slowed as he approached, his boots crunching over something brittle and organic. The sound echoed faintly inside his helmet, filtered through the low hum of his suit's life support system. He didn't look down for long – the ground around the ship was carpeted with it, a soft mat of desiccated growth and pale, fibrous decay that rustled faintly in the breeze.

A note was fixed to the door at eye level.

He peeled it free carefully, gloved fingers steady.

The page was stiff, the stain dark and uneven, soaked deep into the fibres. The handwriting was rough, the letters slanted and unsteady – written in haste, in pain, or both.

He read it once.

Then again.

He would've recognised that handwriting anywhere.

His thumb drifted to the smeared print beneath the final line, tracing the arc of a bloody fingerprint without realising he was doing it. The pressure of it. The weight of it.

The signal from the *Astraea* had been sent over seven months ago. The *Hermes* had been in lightdrift at the time, travelling too fast for any signals to be received. When they dropped out on the outskirts of the HDX-2719 system and had finally discovered the emergency beacon, they sent Erik and a team to *Planet B* to investigate further.

Behind him, the retrieval shuttle sat powered down in the shadow of a rocky ridge, its hull dim beneath the dying light. Beyond that, far above the sky itself, he watched as the *Hermes* continued on towards HDX-2719-c – *Planet C* – exactly as the original mission had intended.

No one had understood why the *Astraea* had deviated from the course at all.

He folded the note with care and slipped it into the inner pocket of his suit, over his heart – as if it might keep her close to him once again.

I have to find her.

The last image of her rose unbidden.

Eva, standing in the airlock. Her long sun-gold hair pulled back into a rough ponytail. The way she'd frowned as he fitted her helmet, his fingers lingering just a moment too long at her jaw. He'd told her he loved her – not because it was dramatic, and not because it was goodbye, but because years together had been enough for him to know he would spend the rest of his life choosing her.

So he'd hit the manual override without hesitation and had felt the pressure of the abyss tear him away – *away from her* – and had welcomed the violence of it, knowing she would live. Knowing that if one of them had to be lost to the great beyond, it should be him.

What he hadn't known was that he would survive.

That within ten seconds he would slip through the escape pod access forcefield instead of drifting into oblivion. That the warnings he'd barely registered before the airlock sealed – elevated solar activity, radiation spikes from an unexpected coronal mass ejection – would cascade into something far worse.

There had been no one assigned to that bay until planetfall. No comms. No override. No way back inside, so he had launched alone – a ghost in a pod – and months later had been found by the NG *Hermes*, pulled half dead from the dark.

Erik lifted his gaze to the horizon.

The valley stretched outward in rolling layers of shadow and mist, and beyond it, a vast belt of green unfurled – dense, tangled, alive. Massive fronds and twisted trunks drank in the last light as HDX-2719 dipped lower, the sky bruising from gold to red.

That's when he saw them – points of pink light stirring at the forest's edge.

At first they drifted slowly, almost beautiful – like dust caught in a slow updraft. Then they multiplied. Thickened. Spilled outward from the trees as dusk deepened, their movement purposeful now, drawn by something unseen.

Erik took a step back, stepping on something near the doorway.

He moved his foot back and noticed something glinting in the dust. Stooping down to pick it up, he held it to the final light as the burnished colour of gold, along with the hint of red and blue almost glowed.

His ring. The one he'd given to Eva.

She was here.

Or she had been...

The light thinned, the sky deepening to midnight blue as the Milky Way emerged overhead – a cold spill of stars – while a thin smear of blood-red lingered at the horizon as the sun slipped away.

And with the darkness came sound.

Distant at first.

Then closer.

In the gloom, shapes shifted, moving towards him with a jerking, unnatural rhythm.

Erik tucked the ring and note inside his breast pocket of his vest, and pulled up his gun, turning once more to the ship's doors. To the place where Eva had stood. To the warning she'd left behind.

He turned again towards the shuttle as its emergency beacons flickered on, casting stark white beams pulsing across the ground.

Screams broke out all around him.

His team.

The sounds tore through the air – ragged and panicked – and for a split second his attention snapped, instinct dragging him to turn back and help his squad.

The pink orbs drifted closer to him now, their glow pulsing softly along the ground as he stepped forwards.

His boot scuffed against the soil – then sank into something wet.

He froze.

Looking down, he saw a wide ring of pale green ferns encircling him, fronds slowly unfurling as soft luminescent spores drifted upward – growing from the swollen, dark mass beneath his feet.

Low growls rippled through the air as darkness finally claimed the world.

Then, his wrist comm unit crackled – a single, static laced message cutting through the eerie quiet.

'Calder, Commander Konrad from the Hermes.'

Static again.

'New orders – return to ship.'

Erik's breath caught as he waited out the static again.

'We found the survivors... Erik—we found Eva.'

His fingers fumbled at the device, hope flaring briefly in his chest. He stepped forward again – but the shadows surrounded him. There was no path ahead. No escape.

Erik lifted his head, clutching the note over his heart – Eva's words echoing in his mind as the light bled from the world.

"If you cannot leave – follow the sun."

He looked around.

There was nothing left to follow.

A NOTE FROM THE AUTHOR

To my best friend, Emma – thank you for the most beautiful twenty-plus years of friendship.

For every late-night conversation, every moment of encouragement, every meltdown you've talked me through, for introducing me to metal, and for holding my hair back. I genuinely cannot imagine this life without you beside me. *In this life or the next. You're stuck with me.*

To my beta readers: Nikki, Paige, Leah, Brendan, Hannah, and Matt – thank you for your early feedback, encouragement, and insight. I hope this final version has made you all proud.

To my street team: you incredible humans have been the heart, hype, and chaos behind *Dead Horizon*. Thank you not only for helping spread the word about this book, but for showing up every single day with excitement, kindness, and unwavering support. Watching you all scream over teasers, quotes, updates, and even some random pictures of steak (IYKYK), has made this journey even more special.

@brendanarnold @thelabrarian @benjamintwiggwrites @leahbrary @raccoon.reader_ @sami.bookstagram @danni.reads.books @danisbooklife @_devourer.of.words @ashleymarascowrites @cosmics.library @brittmccarthy @kelsbookreads @aratecla_the_bookrat @kpkilbrideauthor and @unremarcable_reader.

If you're on social media, please give these wonderful people a follow!

A special thank you to @whatpaigeyreads for managing my street team and somehow matching – and often exceeding – my own level of excitement for every announcement, reveal, and milestone along the way.

To two of the best friends this author journey has given me; fellow authors Brendan Arnold and Benjamin Twigg. Your friendship has become one of the greatest gifts to come from all of this. The constant support, encouragement, advice, and kindness you both offer so freely means more to me than I could ever put into words, and no this will not be the last time I thank you both for all that you do.

And finally, to every reader who has picked up this story – thank you for giving *Dead Horizon* a place in your mind.

Supporting indie authors changes lives more than you probably realise, and I will never take that support for granted.

ABOUT THE AUTHOR

Rachel Jones is an Australian speculative fiction author writing emotionally driven science fiction and horror. Her work explores grief, human morality, and survival through collapsing worlds and encounters with the unknown.

Born and raised in Western Australia, Rachel grew up surrounded by bushland and wide night skies. Her love of space, nature, and storytelling was deeply shaped by her older brother, who first encouraged her to look up at the stars and wonder about what lay beyond them – an influence that continues to guide her writing today.

Rachel writes while balancing full-time work and motherhood, drawing inspiration from the people she loves and the emotional bonds that connect us all.

You can follow her on Instagram at @racheljonesauthor or visit her website: www.racheljonesauthor.com

ALSO BY THE AUTHOR

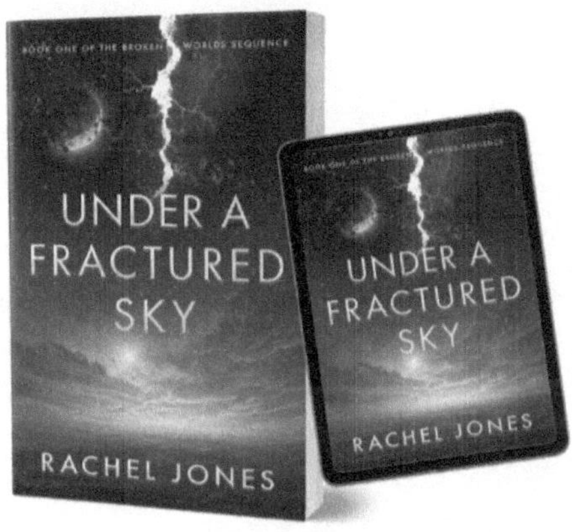

The universe is tearing.

The year is 2180. In the aftermath of global collapse, PANGAEA rebuilt Earth with the promise of order, while hiding a festering reality. Dr Lilliana Hayes lives for the stars and her daughter, but when she uncovers a devastating secret, everything changes.

The Big Rip isn't just a theory anymore.

Blackmailed into helping complete the Gateway – a portal to another universe – Lily is horrified to learn the true cost of survival. As reality fractures and time distorts, she wonders if peace lies not in escape, but in letting go.

Under a Fractured Sky is an apocalyptic sci-fi thriller told through interweaving perspectives, where the greatest threat isn't the end of the universe, but what humanity will do to outrun it.

www.ingramcontent.com/pod-product-compliance
Lightning Source LLC
Chambersburg PA
CBHW030540130726
48054CB00020B/111

* 9 7 8 1 7 6 4 1 0 0 3 2 8 *